Please return/renew this item by
Charges will be made for items re
renewed by telephone or via "e-li
www.bexley.gov.uk/libraries. You
number and PIN. You can also u
library catalogue and reserve iten

C000242359

07/11
Central Library
02083037777

1 5 OCT 2018

30109 05219923 2

Proudly published by Snowbooks

Copyright © 2016 Mark Morris

Snowbooks Ltd.
email: info@snowbooks.com
www.snowbooks.com.

British Library Cataloguing in Publication Data.
A catalogue record for this book is available
from the British Library.

Paperback: 978-1-911390-98-5
Ebook: 978-1-911390-99-2

ALBION FAY

Mark Morris

MADE IN ENGLAND

An Introduction to Albion Fay

ADAM NEVILL

As a quick aside, we British are the world's most haunted people. Most of the world's canon of supernatural fiction is written in English, and most of that was written by the English. On that note, the very first word of this short novel is "Albion": the old name of England. And it is Britishness, and a participation in the British tradition of the supernatural in fiction, that haunts and defines this chilling, tragic and transporting story from, literally, the first word.

Having spent a significant amount of time living in another country, I've often wondered if I have been afforded an outsider's point-of-view of the United Kingdom. Without the wide, open spaces and the vast skies of North America or Australasia, I think there is a peculiar and particular claustrophobia and containment within the visions of British writers, not least its writers of horror. The very culture, the social hierarchy, and the land's over-crowdedness may have partitioned and subdivided the islands into enclosed but, somehow, too visible spaces. As a kingdom in the writer's imagination the country may resemble a three storey Edwardian terrace, a Victorian Gothic Revival townhouse, or a post-war block of flats; a myriad caves often filled with paranoia, petty cruelties, spite, resentment, judgemental competitiveness that peeks over garden fences, and all flourishing in competitive environments like a social bacteria. Mark Morris most comfortably and fluently tells his stories through observations of the pressures and gravities of this society, inflicted by anything from admonishing looks, assumptions of persecution, to the fists of brutes. And British horror itself is often concerned with domesticity and where it rubs against diminishing vestiges of the wild and the ruined that still exhibit a concentration of ancient supernormal powers or presences. It is the musculature of much British horror. And *Albion Fay* flexes those muscles beneath flesh unused to sunlight.

Glimmers of a seventies English idyll in the story are dimmed pretty quickly by the spectre of drunkenness and domestic violence — I could almost see the shape of an enraged, Northern, working class father rising behind a semi-opaque shield of dimpled glass that divides a narrow kitchen from a dim dining room. Our narrator in this story, Frank, also represents the terrible entrapment and impotency within the last two hundred years of England and Englishness, that has been capable of crushing the sensitive individual. The very fear of mortification and public shame, of simply making a fuss, can even handicap the right-thinking to incapacity.

I'm often struck by how many British horror writers populate their stories with the mundane aspects of *the* culture too — it can approach the forensic but has a significant role beyond mere scene setting; it's an interpretation of cultural memory and national temperament, post-empire, and I can think of no better example in English literature than the work of the English poet, Phillip Larkin. There are times when I wonder if all English writers must, at some point, descend to their hands and knees in order to go round and round in a room not papered yellow, but the grey of the over-boiled cabbage of a school dinner. Despite its PR, the climate of the British Isles can fade anything to grey for most of the year, including the spirits of those within its damp borders. In *Albion Fay* too, the familiar is looked upon both with nostalgic familiarity, but also with a morbid detachment that borders on distaste. In doing so, *Albion Fay* takes its place amongst the horror of Nigel Kneale, Ramsey Campbell, Robert Aickman, M John Harrison, even M R James — some of our most deservedly lauded practitioners of the weird tale, who all evoke the strange, enigmatic and ghastly among the dull beiges and greys. In hindsight, the English tradition of horror, in my mind, takes the form of old papers stacked neatly behind a dusty sherry decanter, left in an old sideboard that has been in the family for generations; an article of furniture that sucks all of the light out of the room in which it has settled. But these old papers are filled with secrets that will make your hair stand on end.

Such tendencies in writers must come from the multi-layering of British history and its artefacts that crowd our field of vision, the bewildering class system and its vast divisions, that long ladder where few will ever move from one rung to the next. In *Albion Fay*, and in most of Morris's work that I have read, there exists a most Larkenesque resignation to fate, and a relishing of small comforts. Here we have Sheffield Utd football games and memories of Larry Grayson on the telly, bickering mums and dads, the terror of being branded a sissy at school, the scream of *Doctor Who's* opening credits on a *Satdee* afternoon. Great isn't it? It's what home is? Horrible too. It's why so many British teenagers since the forties have wished they'd been American, or at least Australian from the nineties onwards. And as a reader of *Albion Fay*, so suggestive are the signifiers of British family life in this text (deeply dysfunctional though not in appearance), I found myself bringing my own images from the 1970s to the table:

Quality Street chocolates on special occasions, a gas fire glowing in a corner, the steel front like the grill of an old car, a Nan's rock cakes cooling on a tea towel, grey school uniforms, Morecambe and Wise on the box at Christmas, allotments, school dinners, the seemingly perpetual smell of wet leaves in Autumn that inhabits my memory, a grandfather's fishing trophies, velour chairs, dimpled glass, rumours in the street, hushed voices, twitching nets ...

Mark Morris's Britishness, his comforts and a suppressed uneasiness at these comforts, inhabits the very rooms of his writing as well as informing the timbre of his writing voice. I am not invoking ridicule by mentioning this, but labour this point to highlight Mark Morris as a significant player in the modern folk tradition that is contained in British horror.

As Frank enters a funeral he describes himself in a way that most visitors to England, and consumers of English culture, would immediately identify as English: "I am a neat, unassuming, self-contained man. I like routine, precision, order. I like to be in control of my environment." This thoroughness of characterisation is another Morris trait that is evident in *Albion Fay*. By page ten I have a complete picture of this man, Frank, though am thrown off-kilter by his asexuality and made a trifle uncomfortable by his tendency to self-justify an introverted and reclusive existence. Quiet, undemonstrative, with a default-setting of melancholy, but such people are, to me, always more intriguing in shelves of fiction obsessed with action men and go-getters, lawyers, cops and glamour pusses, bitches and rakes. It's a welcoming gust of stale air from the bottom of an airing cupboard on a first floor landing in a three bedrooms semi', to see a secondary school teacher in slippers shuffling toward his own private edges in a life of quiet desperation. For me, no one writes this character as well as the British. They give it authenticity.

Like so many of the more tremulous, inhibited and ordinary men and women of British horror, from M R James's scholars onwards, there's an immediate sense of a timeworn status quo in Frank, holding people in their place, as well as a terror of making an exhibition of oneself on a crowded island. This leads us to suspect that such characters will feel the coming horrors more acutely (and acute will be their undoings at the hands of such too).

I've always found and enjoyed the sensitivity and vulnerability that exists in Mark Morris's point of view characters, that too few cultivate in the field of horror these days. Too few writers have the same *feel* for them. The late Joel Lane was masterly in this vein, as is Ramsey Campbell.

Morris's narrators, therefore, are often open-eyed wonderers of what the ordinary suddenly appears to mean, or suggest. The ordinary objects, people and situations that crowd us and our memories, develop a second life in his work, and become more curious as if they might conceal awful revelations for the beholder. And so the suggested truths in *Albion Fay* also gather a momentum that forms as much of a story as the events themselves. And behind the action, the metronome of pace - that is placed upon that old, brown sideboard - ticks steadily, undemonstratively, but insistently.

In Albion Fay, we have strong examples of the trademark Morris subtlety and writerly senses, finely tuned to nuances of social vibrations, of objects that retain echoes. He is at his best when he is pondering and making subtle reflections.

"I stare at the coffin directly in front of me, no more than a dozen steps away, and it strikes me that its occupant is one person no longer contributing to the heat in the room. In fact, I think, there is not even a person in there any more. There is simply an absence, an empty receptacle, as cold as the glass against which the dark clouds press, as senseless as the wooden cross on the wall."

There are so many ways in which our fear and distaste for death can manifest in horror. Here's an example of one of the better ways, which reminds me of Larkin in his *Whitsun Wedding* days, and which is quintessentially Morris, and English:

"The mourners will all be outside now, reading the notes on the flowers, gossiping, looking at their watches. How long before they move on, glad to get this over with, put this day behind them?"

On the matter of narrative, there is a suppressed and effective set-up here that doesn't chime a single false note: a sad and lonely man at a funeral, then a timid excavation of old photographs that reveal a cave system from a distant family holiday. And immediately we feel the caves will lead us right back to that funeral, only we cannot guess how. The story telling, like the characterisation, is neat, meticulous, precise, steadily paced and fastidious. I sense a considered mind behind a slow moving pen; in an age of speed, of cognitive overloads, of entertainment bombardment, it feels good to slip into a lower narrative gear. And the horrors we feel will mostly be contained in the confines of the greatest and darkest cave of all: the mind.

"My bed feels unfamiliar and the darkness around me smells

odd, like soil. I hear a rushing sound, as if a distant crowd of people is all whispering at once."

The forebodings and the hints of the unnatural are quintessentially British too, because we must remember that the grounds of olde Albion near writhe with the shrivelled remains from wars and plagues, executions and invasions. Our very ancestral memory is incomplete without the spectre of skeletal death:

"Beside it, tall and elongated, is something so solidly black that I'm certain it must be a figure. I imagine the figure staring at me, imagine malevolence uncoiling from it, like the unfurling legs of a vast black spider."

From M R James, De La Mare to Wakefield, and on to Ramsey Campbell and Reggie Oliver, our reactions to the ghastly remain intact after two world wars and the economy's destruction of what Britain appeared to be in the seventies. This, for instance, could have been written in the 1920s (and that is no bad thing):

"My fear is not tempered, however, but merely diverted; the widening wedge of grey, the thin creak that accompanies it, means that my door is opening. I see a narrow streak of darkness haloed by the grey and this time I know it *is* a figure."

Albion Fay also explores the same ancient earthworks and myths of Machen's *The White People*, Ramsey Campbell's *The Kind Folk*, and Neil Marshall's *The Descent* (surely one of the best British horror films of the last twenty years). But in *Albion Fay* we have the "night people" not the white people. The cave itself is another powerful symbol and entity in literature. The cave features a timeless dark, one often unchanged for vast stretches of time we cannot comprehend; but these are features of the earth that are capable of changing *that* which ventures inside walls long predating our sentience. From E M Forster's caves in *A Passage to India* to the subterranean pathways in Ramsey Campbell's *The Darkest Part of the Woods*, and Machen's ancient gateways in *The Shining Pyramid*, the British often call upon the old landscapes and what they hide, those things beyond modernity and its sophistications, that are far older than Christianity, and often beyond our understanding of good and evil.

Another quintessential trademark of the best in British horror is the turn of phrase that is used when presenting the uncanny to the reader's imagination. It is a craft and artfulness that is chief in suspending reader disbelief and ensuring that stories endure, at least in the reader's mind. The Victorian and Edwardian purveyors of terror set and left a very high standard for their descendants to maintain. For me, I can't read horror that lacks this literary quality. The effective turn of phrase is the hallmark of a writer's eye for the sublime in terror. Here are two of Mark Morris's choice contributions to this tradition:

"For a few minutes I listen to the wind in the trees. I know the sound isn't a voice, but it sounds like one that keeps collapsing on the verge of forming words."

"My thoughts feel heavy and dull, as if the illness that has devoured the memories of so many in this room is now beginning to affect me as well."

What we often remember of horror are the forces incrementally conjured by the writer; the sense of supernormal energy building, without rising too far too fast, and how the reader is transported by that writer's tactical passages of description. Here are two more examples:

"She says the sound of that laughing up in the trees was the worst thing she'd ever heard."

"In fact, the longer I stare at the caves the more I imagine something with flat, cold, unblinking eyes staring back at me from the shadows.

They get angry if you look at them, Scott said."

The reveal, if it comes, is the greatest risk in stories so carefully constructed (and mostly out of memory and a nonlinear timescale in this case). I think the risk here was both well-judged and well taken. When we get a better look at the "night people", we wish we hadn't, and the novella scrapes against the parts of the Lovecraftian tradition (that was also influenced by the British tradition of the weird and fantastic). In this case, there are echoes of Machen's hideous ancient races and what inhabits Hodgson's Borderland:

"It's maggot-white and its skin glistens, gleams. It's thin and shaped like a man, but it seems boneless, sliding along the rock wall as if moulding itself like a jellyfish to the rough bulges and jags and crevices. It has no face that I can see, but behind the featureless, gelid mask something shifts and swirls. It reminds me of the constantly changing colours in an oil slick and it seems to possess a queasy and dreadful significance.

They bite"

Biology and geology seem to infuse the horror and the last vestiges of any Victorian interpretations of fairy folk are immediately banished. There is more of the blind and insistent slug, or the life-draining leech, than an angelic figure with gossamer wings. The caves regress us and reveal their atavistic nature, they prod our reptilian brain, and the impermanence and insignificance of our status as enlightened modern men and women, is suddenly confronted by tens of millions of years of convulsions in the very earth, of monstrous food chains and the cruel legacies of nature that we can only be aghast at and horrified by.

Anyway, I won't keep you any longer, the night people are calling from the mouths of old caves. Lose yourself in a fine story of loss — the loss of memory, the loss of parental love, the loss of the beloved, and the loss of one's self underground and in the wider world. At the borders of such loss place yourself before these omens and portents. Through this opening in the ground of old England, allow yourself to be led unto a place where natural law has no tyranny. But no screaming please, we're British.

Or at least muffle your shrieks with handfuls of soil, or some old bed sheets.

ADAM NEVILL (BIRMINGHAM AND DEVON 2014).

ALBION FAY

Mark Morris

I am determined to hold it together, but as soon as I enter the crematorium chapel the reality of the situation hits me all over again and I feel as if my innards have been scooped out, as if my body has suddenly been transformed from a fleshy, weighty thing to something brittle and hollow. I go cold inside, but conversely I start to sweat. My vision blurs and the walls of the room seem to buckle inwards, like a paper bag in the process of having the air sucked out of it.

Do I make a sound? Totter or stumble? I don't know, but I'm certainly aware of heads turning, of eyes fixing on me. Perhaps they're staring not because I'm making a scene, but because of my current situation. Not all of them can know, of course, but I'm sure some of them have formed their own opinions, doubtless based on half-facts and hearsay. What do they think I've done, some of them? I shudder to think. Or at least, I *would* shudder if I really cared. Death has a way of making even our most serious concerns seem trivial by comparison.

Expelling a long breath, I blink to clear my vision. Raising my head to focus on the large wooden cross affixed to the wall, and on the pair of high, square windows above it, across which roll bruised and boiling clouds, I move steadily down the aisle between the two blocks of seats packed with black-clad mourners. Some are weeping quietly, their wet sniffs and sharp hitches of breath reverberating off the walls, as if the chapel has been specifically designed to amplify and accentuate grief. Others whisper or

1

murmur to their neighbours as I pass by, and though I hear no words, I'm aware of a rising susurration, like wind in the trees that presages an approaching storm.

Ignoring them all, I take my place on the front row. I don't realize I am sitting next to Chris's mum until she reaches out and grabs my hand. Squeezing it tightly enough to make my bones hurt, she leans towards me, the black lace on her hat rustling like a restless snake.

"Why did this happen, Frank?" she says. "What sort of God..." But then grief overcomes her and her voice chokes off.

"I don't know," I whisper as the sobs she is coughing up make her body jerk and sag. Perhaps she expects more from me, but I can't offer it. Even if my throat hadn't closed off, strangling my voice, I wouldn't know what to say. I am all out of insight, all out of comfort. I feel as though I have dwindled to nothing. In a way I am surprised she is able to see me at all.

The ceremony is a blur. Afterwards I can't recall who has spoken, what has been said. When it's over I remain in my seat as the shuffling rumble behind me announces that people are standing up, moving towards the exit. It is the first cold day of autumn — I saw conkers lying on the path as I walked up from the car park through the trees earlier, and a hook of bitter-sweet nostalgia plucked me instantly back to childhood — yet the interior of the chapel has grown stuffy as the ceremony has progressed, warmed by the beat of life and the outpouring of mostly-stifled emotion. Sitting in the fug of perfume and floor polish, sweat scurrying like insects' feet down my back and belly, I stare at the coffin directly in front of me, no more than a dozen steps away, and it strikes me that its occupant is one person no longer contributing to the heat in the room. In fact, I think, there is not even a person in there any more. There is simply an absence, an empty receptacle, as cold as the glass against which the dark clouds press, as senseless as the wooden cross on the wall.

The thought horrifies me, especially as I recall how alive she had been. In my mind she is a little girl again, running and laughing, her eyes sparkling, the sun glowing on her skin. She is happy in my memory; she seems immortal. It is inconceivable that all that life has been snuffed out for ever, that her days are done so soon.

I wait until the rumbling and shuffling and low, murmured conversation has dwindled to silence. I remain seated even when I know I am alone, my body bent forward at the waist, my elbows propped on my knees. I keep my head down and my eyes closed, resting my forehead on the knuckles of my clasped hands, effectively sealing myself off from the world. The mourners will all be outside now, reading the notes on the flowers, gossiping, looking at their watches. How long before they move on, glad to get this over with, put this day behind them?

A song plays softly over the speakers. It must have been playing for a while, repeated on a loop as the congregation filed out of the building, but I have been too preoccupied to register it. Now it worms into my consciousness, and although the song was my own suggestion I shock myself by bursting into tears. Even as my shoulders hitch and the tears trickle over my clenched fists and drip to the floor, there is a small part of me that feels embarrassed, even ashamed, of my outburst. Here I am, having remained stoical throughout the ceremony, suddenly reduced to mush by Whitney Houston's *I Will Always Love You*. If this was a scene in a movie, it would seem mawkish, schmaltzy. But to me, sitting alone in a deserted chapel, it all at once seems unbearably poignant.

I try to stem the flow of tears, but they keep pouring out of me. I am crying not just because of what has happened, but because I should have seen it coming, should have prevented it. The signs have been there for years, for decades; with hindsight the conclusion, in many ways, is inevitable. I see now that it has been an accumulation of events, each a marker on a journey that started at Albion Fay.

I am so wrapped up in my grief that I don't realize I have company. The first I am aware of it is when I feel the gentle pressure of a hand on my shoulder. Shock spasms through my body and I jerk upright, my eyes snapping open, my vision instantly blurring with unshed tears. I am suddenly certain that she will be there beside me, that my emotions have been so intense that I have somehow called her back.

But of course that isn't the case. Even through my swimming vision I see that the figure beside me is tall and thin, the pale smudge of its head topped by a cloudy blur of grey hair. I unmesh my hands and knuckle tears from my eyes. The sallow, beaky-nosed face of Reverend Howard comes into focus as he begins to speak.

"I'm so sorry to intrude. I just wondered whether I could be of any help?"

His voice is warm, husky, solicitous. I wonder, perhaps uncharitably, whether he has interrupted my grief as a prelude to ushering me out of the building, so that he can prepare for the next funeral.

I shake my head. "No, no," I say, "I'm all right. It's just..." I feel my voice tightening and pause. He smiles.

"Yes?"

"This song. It's stupid I know, but it suddenly just... got to me."

He tilts his head, as though straining to catch a hint of elusive birdsong on the air. "Ah," he says non-commitally.

I blunder on, annoyed with myself for feeling I have to explain. "Yes, it was always Angie's favourite, you see. Angharad, I mean. My sister."

*

The box is waiting for me when I get home.

This is not a surprise, of course. I was the one who put it on the low table in front of the settee. I removed it from Angie's house the last time I was there, a few days ago, but I haven't been able to face opening it before now. I wanted to get today's funeral out of the way first. I knew that it was going to be an ordeal and I didn't want to... well, weaken myself beforehand.

Now that I'm all cried out, though, now that I'm as drained and raw as I feel I can possibly be, I'm ready — or as ready as I ever will be. It'll be hard, I know that, but I don't think it can make me feel any worse than I already do. On the contrary, opening the box might well be cathartic, a comfort even, a reminder of happier times. And if it *does* prove too painful... well, I can always close it again.

As soon as I unlock the door of my little house and step into the hallway I feel the box calling to me. A mental itch that I know I will have to scratch. Even so, I take my time, working my way round to it. I take off my damp coat — it is drizzling outside now — and hang it on one of a row of pegs behind the front door. I slip off my shiny black shoes, which I only wear to weddings and funerals, and which never fail to rub my heels, and step thankfully into my slippers. I tug off my tie and undo the top button of my shirt, which is pressing against my Adam's apple. Then, bypassing the front room on my left, I walk to the end of the short hallway and into the kitchen.

I continue to ignore the itch as I make myself a tuna fish sandwich and a mug of tea, adding a spoonful of honey because I have convinced myself it is a healthy alternative to sugar. Before eating, I wipe the kitchen surface, brush crumbs from the bread board into the sink and rinse them away, and wash up the few implements I have used, putting the cutlery back into the drawer and the now-clean tuna can into the correct one of three plastic recycling boxes. When the kitchen is once more spick and span, I stand in front of the small window beside the back door and stare out at the potted shrubs cowering from the rain in my little back garden as I sip my tea and stolidly munch my way through my sandwich. When I am done I wash and dry my plate and mug and put them away.

The garden, and indeed the house in which I have lived for the past twenty-two years, is, I suppose, an extension of me, of who I am. I am a neat, unassuming, self-contained man. I like routine, precision, order. I like to be in control of my environment. I like to keep myself to myself. I have few friends.

That makes me sound boring, I know, and maybe even a bit creepy, but I don't think I'm either of those things. All right, maybe I *am* boring by some people's standards, but there's a world of difference between being boring and being stuffy. I may be something of a control freak, but that doesn't automatically make me a snob. I don't judge other people. I don't cast aspersions on how others choose to run their lives. I'm personable and popular at work. I have a good relationship with both my colleagues and my pupils — or at least, I did until the incident with Tamsin Wicks. Even now I believe that I still have the support of most of the staff, pupils and parents associated with the school, and that it's only a matter of time before I'm reinstated. Everyone knows that the Wicks girl is a troublemaker and that sooner or later her spite will catch up with her. Miss Glasson only suspended me because she had to, because her hands were tied. And she did it with regret. That was the phrase she used when she called me into her office. "With regret, Frank," she said.

But never mind that. The box. The box is waiting for me. I can't ignore the itch any longer. I turn with a heavy heart and walk out of the kitchen, along the corridor and into the front room.

My gran called it a living room and Mum called it a lounge, but to me this has always been the front room. It's where I spend most of my time when I'm at home. I eat my meals in here and watch TV and listen to music and read and browse the internet. I don't watch porn, if you're wondering. I've never felt the need to. Some people think that if you're an unmarried middle-aged man living alone, you must automatically be a bit of a pervert. They probably base their argument on what they would be like if they were in my situation, with nowhere to direct their urges.

But I don't have urges. Not sexual ones anyway. I know that may be hard to believe, but it's true. I'm not gay. I'm not even in denial. I'm just... asexual. I don't know why. Maybe it's because of my parents. Maybe witnessing their relationship on a day to day basis poisoned me, or flipped a switch inside me. Or maybe it's a fluke of nature. Maybe I was born without a particular hormone or chemical. I don't know and it doesn't bother me. It's not something I've ever worried about, or discussed with a psychiatrist, or sought treatment for. In fact, judging by how other people conduct their affairs (if you'll pardon the pun), I would say my 'condition', if you want to call it that, has saved me a great deal of time and hassle.

Just because I don't get 'horny' doesn't mean I don't feel anything, though. I'm not emotionless, I'm not a sociopath. I'd describe myself as a caring, compassionate, understanding person. I love my family, the few that I have. I like most of my work colleagues, and most of the children at the secondary school where I teach English and Drama. I like going to the cinema and the theatre. I laugh at comedies and I get teary-eyed at moments of poignancy in films and books. I hate injustice and bigotry and willful ignorance. I'm sickened by cruelty and violence.

I sit on the settee and look at the box. It's a perfectly ordinary cardboard box, quite large — in fact, the printed lettering on the side proclaims that it once contained a Canon MX455 inkjet printer. It is sealed across the top with a strip of brown parcel tape, which I applied to hold the two flaps together, and also to... I don't know, *contain* the contents somehow, or at least provide a barrier, however flimsy, against temptation. It's not that the contents of the box are volatile — although they are to me.

Clenching my hand briefly to stop it from trembling, I reach out, snag a fingernail under the edge of the tape, and then, bracing myself as if about to remove a dressing from a wound, rip it from the box.

The two sides of the lid rise slightly as if the box, or its contents, is sighing. I screw up the strip of parcel tape in one hand, put it on the table next to the box, and push back one side of the lid, then the other. Inside, stacked one on top of the other, are four albums with thick, spongy, leather-look covers. The topmost one is the oldest, its blue cover dulled by time. The single engraved word slanting across the cover in calligraphy-style lettering reads: 'Photographs'. The gold paint used to highlight the word is chipped and faded.

Almost reverently I lift the album from the box and place it in my lap. As I tilt it slightly, something slips from between its thick, cardboard pages and falls to the floor. I don't see it, but hear the *plip* sound it makes as it hits the carpet, like a fish breaking the surface of a pond. I look down and see a photograph lying face-down, its white back yellowing at the edges. Still balancing the album on my lap, I grunt as I lean forward and pick the photograph up off the floor. For a forty-eight year old man I'm in reasonably good shape — I jog twice a week and sometimes I go to the gym — but in the past few years I have developed a thickening layer of fat around my middle, which no amount of exercise seems able to shift.

My heart is beating fast, though not from the exertion of stretching to pick up the photograph. For a moment I pause, and then I turn the photograph over. It depicts two children. Twins. Both ten. The boy blond-haired, pensive-looking, the girl skinny, boyish, grinning. The boy's hands, fingers curled inwards, are by his sides; the girl, hips tilted at an almost vampish angle as she leans into him, has her arm slung loosely, casually across his shoulders. The boy wears a black, white and green striped polo shirt and blue shorts, the girl a sleeveless purple top and white denim shorts. It is summer; their flawless, brown limbs are dappled by sunlight. They are surrounded by greenery. The grass, sloping up behind them, and the leaves on the trees are so vivid they look almost luminous.

My mouth is so dry I can barely swallow. I know exactly when this photo was taken: July 1975. And I know where it was taken: on the sloping lawn beneath Albion Fay.

The boy in the photograph is me. The girl is my sister, Angie.

This is the morning of the day when we went into the caves for the first time.

It is the day when our lives changed forever.

*

What do we see first? The house or the caves? I don't remember. My impression is that they are the same, that one forms from the other. It is as if the rough, grey, speckled rock has squeezed and honed itself into the shape of something that resembles a house, but that is really a trap for the unwary. Or perhaps it's the other way round; perhaps the rock, pockmarked with caves, which rises in whorls and crags behind the house, are the building's nightmares made manifest, an outpouring of feverish, insane energy that has accumulated, swelled, risen like a leviathan as if to crush the structure below, only to freeze, calcify, its rough surface channeled with deposits of lime, like glimmers of bone pushing up through the skin.

A fanciful notion? Of course. It's wild, melodramatic, ridiculous. But it doesn't alter the fact it's the way I remember it. It's the form it's taken, twisted and monstrous, in my mind these past thirty-eight years.

The approach to the house is like descending into another world. It is as if we have taken a sideways step from humdrum reality into a hidden, ancient realm, murky with dark magic. We miss the turning three times, going back and forth along the road, before we spot it. Our parents become increasingly vicious with one another, each blaming the other for a lack of competence.

But although Angie and I exchange rolling-eyed, grimacing expressions, on this occasion we almost don't care. To us, missing the turning seems almost like a rite of passage. We find out later that we were both thinking the same thing: Only those seeking the way for a fourth time shall find it.

It's Angie who finally spots it. The signpost, rotten and faded, is leaning over and tangled with foliage, which in turn sprawls across the narrow gap between the hedges on either side of the opening. This gives the impression, at first glance, that there *is* no gap, that it is one continuous hedge. It is only because Dad has slowed the car to fifteen miles an hour that Angie sees it on the fourth pass.

"There!" she squeals, pointing.

Dad slows the car to a crawl. The road is twisty and turny, and enclosed by high hedges. If anything comes speeding round the corner now it will smash into the back of us. But nothing does. Dad scowls.

"Where?"

"*There*, George," says Mum. "I see it now too. That dark area, look. And there's the sign. It's just a bit overgrown, that's all."

"A *bit* overgrown?" Dad is still scowling. "If they can't be bothered to make it clear where we're supposed to turn, God knows what the road down to the house will be like. Not to mention the place itself. It's probably a bloody ruin."

He glares at Mum as he says this. She was the one who found the house and booked it. I have no idea *where* she found it, or why she and Dad decided it would be a suitable place for our annual holiday. As a child you don't ask such questions. You just accept the decisions that are made on your behalf.

Grumbling that the thorny branches of the hedge better not

scratch the car, Dad turns into the dark gap that both Mum and Angie have identified. Immediately a green canopy folds over us, admitting dapples of sunlight like a soft tumble of stars. As the car jolts down a dirt track between trees that become larger and more twisted as we progress, Dad hunches over the wheel, wincing each time the car lurches over a particularly jagged bump. Angie and I, though, grin at each other; I see from her expression that she is feeling the same growing tingle of excitement as me, the sense that we are about to embark on an exciting adventure. Mum too, though she casts occasional anxious glances at Dad, starts to smile as she looks out at the greenery surrounding us.

"It's like... what's that place in *The Hobbit*?" she asks.

"Middle Earth," I tell her.

"Yes," she says. "It's like descending into Middle Earth. It's kind of magical, isn't it, George?"

Dad grunts.

She looks exasperated. I can almost hear the words she wants to say before she says them: *For God's sake, George, cheer up! We're supposed to be on holiday!* She glares at Dad for a moment and then she turns away without speaking. We bump along the dirt road in silence for another few minutes, and then the trees on our left abruptly fall away and light from a suddenly bright sky tumbles over us like a waterfall, and Angie, turning towards it, gasps.

It isn't the light that makes her gasp; it's the house and the caves. I scramble along the length of the back seat and lean across her to see what she can see. Directly to our left is a stone wall perhaps four feet high. Rising from the stone wall is a sloping lawn inset with flower beds and occasional crooked, leaning fruit trees, at the top of which is a big stone house with a slate roof. Next to the house, behind it and to the right of it as we look, is what appears to be a huge cliff face blotched with areas of blackness, which are clearly tunnels and caves.

"They're like eyes," Angie breathes, and though there is a thrill of fear in her voice her own eyes are shining. "Eyes in the rock."

Dad brings the car to a halt and looks grumpily up at the house. "How are we supposed to haul our luggage up there?"

Mum points ahead. "There, look. There's a gate and some steps. Go forward a bit, George. There's a little parking area on the right."

The gate, consisting of roughly hewn staves of wood lashed together with wire, has a weathered wooden sign attached to the front of it. The black letters painted on a white background have been almost obliterated by the elements, but they're still readable: Albion Fay.

Angie reads the name quietly to herself. "What does it mean, Mum?"

"Well, Albion is an ancient name for Great Britain. And I think Fay means fairy."

"Britain Fairy," Angie says and wrinkles her nose. "That doesn't make sense."

"Maybe it means British Fairy," I say.

Dad sniggers. "British Fairy? Who owns this place then? Larry bloody Grayson?"

Mum rolls her eyes as Dad guffaws. I laugh uneasily, though I know that the joke he's made is not very nice. Larry Grayson is a comedian on telly who either is, or pretends to be, a homo. I know that a homo is a man who has sex with other men, because a boy at school told me.

I like Larry Grayson, though. I think he's funny, and he seems kind. He makes me laugh when he says 'Shut that door' and 'What a gay day' and 'Look at the muck in here.' I don't laugh when he's on telly if Dad's around, though, because Dad doesn't like him; he seems to make Dad angry. Dad calls him a 'bloody puff' and says that people like that shouldn't be allowed on TV.

Because Larry Grayson makes me laugh, and because of what Dad has said about him, I wonder if *I'm* a homo, or at least whether I'm going to grow up to be one. I sometimes worry that Dad thinks I already am; he's called me a 'cissy' and a 'puff' before, mainly because I don't like football and I'm not very good at it. About five years ago, when I was five, Dad took me to a football match between Sheffield United and Ipswich Town. What I remember most about the experience is feeling confused and a bit scared. I didn't know what was going on and why a lot of the men around me were shouting and getting angry. Then someone scored (although I didn't know that was what had happened at the time) and all the men who'd been shouting suddenly started screaming and jumping in the air and waving their arms about, including my dad. I was so terrified I burst into tears. Dad looked down at me and his face was shining and his eyes were wild with joy. Then his expression changed. All at once he looked disgusted and ashamed. "What are you bloody crying for?" he said. "We've just scored. You should be happy." He never took me to a football match again.

Another time a boy at school pushed me over in the mud. I came home with grazed elbows and filthy clothes. When Dad found out what had happened he came upstairs to my bedroom. I was lying on my bed, reading. I like reading, but Dad always shakes his head when he sees me with a book, as if I'm doing something 'cissy', so I try not to let him catch me at it too often. This time, though, he caught me by surprise. He doesn't normally come into my room. He looked at the book and said, "Put that down for a minute. I want to talk to you." I quickly put my bookmark into my book and put it on my bedside table and scrambled up into a sitting position as he walked over to my bed and sat down. I was nervous. I'm hardly ever alone with Dad, and when I am I'm always on edge because I think I'm going to disappoint him and make him angry.

"What's this I hear about you getting in a fight?" he said.

"I wasn't in a fight," I told him. "A boy pushed me over."

He frowned as if that wasn't what he wanted to hear. "Who is this boy?"

"I don't know. He's older than me."

"How big is he?"

My mind went blank. Did Dad want me to say an exact height? I wasn't even sure how tall *I* was.

Dad's frown turned into a scowl. "What's up? Cat got your tongue?"

"No, I... I just don't know how big he is."

He rolled his eyes. "Well, is he bigger or smaller than you?"

"Bigger."

Dad nodded. "Well, that's okay. You know what they say, don't you?"

Again I stared at him. I didn't know what he wanted me to say, so all I said was, "What?"

"The bigger they are the harder they fall. And they're right. Do you know what that means?"

I nodded.

"Okay," he said. "So here's what I want you to do tomorrow when you go to school. I want you to find this boy and I want you to say, 'Hey, I've got a present for you.' And when he says, 'What?', I want you to say, 'A knuckle sandwich'. And then, before he can think about what you've said, I want you to punch him as hard as you can in the face." He tapped the bony bit near the top of his nose with his index finger. "Hit him here. As hard as you can. Do that and I guarantee he'll never bother you again." He stood up, making the bed bounce, the springs creak. "Don't let people push you around. Always get your retaliation in first." He walked to the door, but before going out he turned back to me. "What are you going to do tomorrow?"

My throat was dry. I felt utterly miserable. "Hit the boy in the face."

He cupped a hand behind his ear. "Speak up. I can't hear you."

I cleared my throat. "Hit the boy in the face."

I was in a blind panic for the rest of the evening. I didn't know what to do. I didn't want to hit the boy in the face. I was too scared of what would happen to me if I did. But if I didn't hit the boy in the face I was certain that my dad would find out, and I was as scared of him as I was of the boy and his friends. I couldn't eat, couldn't concentrate. After tea I went upstairs and lay on my bed, trying not to cry. At last Mum came up and asked if I was all right, and when I said that I was, she said, "Are you upset because of what happened at school today?"

"Sort of," I said.

Eventually she wheedled out of me what Dad had said, and when she did she got really angry. "That man!" she said. "Don't listen to your father, Frank. Don't you dare do what he says!"

"I won't," I said, relieved. "But won't Dad be angry with me?"

"Let him try," she said. "He'll have to come through me to get to you."

"I don't want *you* to get hurt," I said, alarmed, and she laughed.

"Don't you worry about me," she said. "I can take care of myself."

I pleaded with her not to tell Dad I'd told her, and again she told me not to worry. Even so, I spent the next few days in a state of terror, thinking it would be only a matter of time before Dad brought the subject up again, thinking he would be bound to ask whether I'd taken his advice and punched the bigger boy in the face.

But he didn't ask. He seemed to forget all about it. Or maybe Mum had a word with him; maybe her influence over him was greater than I thought. If so, it must have been something that happened behind closed doors, out of sight and earshot of Angie and me.

We get out of the car and stretch and look up at the house. Then Dad opens the boot and calls us over to grab our bags. He throws my bag at me hard as if testing my strength. It's quite a big bag — an Adidas sports bag stuffed with clothes and books — and it scrapes my arm as I catch it and a sharp, hard corner hits me in the chest and causes pain to flare in my breast bone. I stagger back a few steps, but I manage to hold on to the bag and stay on my feet. My chest and arm hurt enough to make hot, stuffy tears rise to the backs of my eyes, but I refuse to cry in front of Dad. He grins, but I don't know whether that's because he's pleased with me or because he thinks that throwing my bag at me and trying to knock me over is funny. I turn towards the house and kick open the gate and start plodding up the winding, uneven stone steps, diverting my pain and my upset into anger and energy.

Angie is already at the top and has put her bag down by the front door. Outside the door is a sort of wooden platform on thick stilts, which have been sunk into the uneven ground in such a way that it keeps the platform level. On the platform, which is surrounded on all sides by a wooden hand-rail that makes it look like the deck of a ship, is some outdoor furniture and a mobile barbecue. Angie leads me to the edge of the platform overlooking the garden and points at a couple of things you can only see from this high up: a hammock slung between two trees next to a leafy hedge on the right-hand side of the garden, and a mass of woodland sprawling away on the opposite side of the road from the house, from which a tall red-brick chimney sticks up from a thick canopy of trees.

"I want to explore!" she declares.

Mum, who is huffing up the steps with a suitcase in one hand and a bag of groceries in the other, overhears her.

"There'll be plenty of time for that tomorrow. First we need to unpack and then I need you to help me make dinner."

Angie pouts. "Can't me and Frank explore the caves while *you* make dinner?"

"Not tonight," Mum says. "It's nearly seven as it is. By the time we're done it'll be getting dark."

"But Mum!" Angie says.

"Do as you're told, girl!" Dad barks, stomping up the steps with a bag in each hand and another under each arm, as if to prove how strong he is. "It's been a long day. Your mother's tired. Don't be so bloody selfish"

Angie reddens. Mum says, "She wasn't being selfish, George. She's just excited. They both are. It's understandable."

Dad glares at her. "Well, pardon me for sticking up for you. I won't bloody bother in future."

He drops the bags with a clatter on the wooden decking and lifts the flap of a small wooden box sitting behind a shrub in a plant pot beside the front door. As he lifts out a set of keys, Mum looks at us, raises her eyebrows and smiles resignedly.

I smile back and feel guilty for wishing that Dad had not been able to get the time off work and that only me, Angie and Mum were here.

*

When I wake up I don't know where I am. My bed feels unfamiliar and the darkness around me smells odd, like soil. I hear a rushing sound, as if a distant crowd of people is all whispering at once. I raise my head and look towards the sound, my eyes drawn by a patch of dimness, which is a shade or two lighter than the blackness around it. Am I underground? I think of a grave, of soil pattering on a coffin lid, and of how that might sound from the inside. At once I feel stifled, unable to breathe. I struggle into a sitting position, sweating, panicking, clawing at the collar of my pyjamas. "No," I croak, "no, don't..." The patch of dimness seems to waver. Beside it, tall and elongated, is something so solidly black that I'm certain it must be a figure. I imagine the figure staring at me, imagine malevolence uncoiling from it, like the unfurling legs of a vast black spider. I am frozen with terror. I hear the presence sigh, as if in regret.

The sigh becomes a thin, high squeal as a line of grey appears and widens beside the figure. Although the greyness is not exactly light, it spills into the space around it, diluting the darkness, and I realize that I'm enclosed not in a grave but a room. The patch of dimness, I see now, is a window; the black presence is a tall wardrobe. The sound I can hear is neither whispering nor soil pattering on a coffin lid, but only the rush of wind in the trees, the leaves and branches scraping and creaking as they move.

My fear is not tempered, however, but merely diverted; the

widening wedge of grey, the thin creak that accompanies it, means that my door is opening. I see a narrow streak of darkness haloed by the grey and this time I know it *is* a figure.

"Who's there?" I hiss, pushing the words up and out of my lungs and throat with difficulty, as if they are lumps of stone.

"It's me," comes the answer, and all at once I remember fully where I am. The tension seeps out of me as my sister pushes the door shut and pads across the room. She lifts the covers and crawls into bed, shuffling up next to me.

"What do you want?" I ask.

"I don't want to be on my own," she says.

"Why not? Are you scared?" I scoff, then immediately feel appalled; for a split-second I sound like Dad.

"Course not." She is silent for a moment. Then she says, "Mum and Dad were arguing again. I don't like it. It makes me sad."

I listen, but all I hear is the wind in the trees. "I don't hear them."

"They've stopped now."

I lie down, facing away from Angie. She attaches herself limpet-like to my back.

"Your feet are cold," I say.

Already her voice is drowsy. "They'll warm up in a minute."

We lie there, clamped together like one person, her arms curled beneath mine, her hands on my chest, our legs entwined.

For a few minutes I listen to the wind in the trees. I know the sound isn't a voice, but it sounds like one that keeps collapsing on the verge of forming words. There's a screech far away in the night, then I think I hear something scratching at the window. When I raise my head an inch or two from the pillow to listen, the sound stops.

Slowly lowering my head again, I ask, "What were they arguing about?"

"What?"

"Mum and Dad. What were they arguing about?"

She doesn't answer straight away and when she does her voice is reluctant. "You mostly."

I feel something in my stomach tighten. "Me?"

"Mmm."

"Why?"

She sighs. Her breath is warm on my neck. Her body radiates heat. "It doesn't matter."

"It *does* matter," I say. "What did they say?"

She sighs. "Dad was just being horrible as usual. I think he was drunk. Mum was sticking up for you."

My heart is thumping so hard I feel sick. "What was he saying about me?"

"I can't remember."

"You *can* remember."

"I *can't.*"

I lie there, nauseous and miserable. Do I hate my dad? I don't know. I suppose I mustn't do, because if I hated him would I care what he thought of me?

Do I love him then? I don't know that either. If I say no will that make me a bad person? I love Mum and Angie, and they love me, but I don't know if Dad loves me, and that makes me feel worse than anything I can think of.

I think Angie has fallen asleep, but then she whispers, "Are you okay?"

"Yes," I say.

After a moment she says, "You know Lizzie Parkes at school?"

"Who?"

"Lizzie Parkes. Her brother's in that pop group."

"What about her?" I say.

She hesitates, then says, "She told me how to make boys happy."

I wonder what this has to do with anything. "What do you mean?"

"She told me that if you hold a boy's willy in your hand and rub it really hard it makes them happy."

I don't know what to say, so I just say, "Oh."

"Do you want me to make *you* happy, Frank?" Angie asks. "I'll do it if you want me to. I want you to be happy."

I feel a curl of something in my belly. "No," I say, "that's okay."

"Are you sure?" she says. "I don't mind."

"No," I say again.

*

"It's darker than you think it'll be, isn't it?"

Angie, who has moved ahead of me, stops and turns. The narrow entrance to the cave is less than thirty metres behind us, but already her slim body is only a little more defined than the shadows around her. Her face is a blurred oval; it is as though the cave is absorbing her. I can't even see a glint of light from her eyes or teeth.

As if the dimness is affecting my balance I put out a hand and touch the rocky wall. It is colder than I expect. Angie's voice, light and gently mocking, echoes off the jagged walls.

"You're not scared are you, little brother?"

"Course not," I say, stung.

It's not her teasing that riles me, it's her use of the word 'little'. Although Angie and I are twins, she is older than me by forty minutes. I don't know why it annoys me when she reminds me of the fact, but it does. Her words are never spiteful and yet whenever she refers to our birth I can't help but feel that she is attempting to assert her superiority, put me in my place. If she knew this was how I felt I'm sure she would be horrified. In all other respects Angie and I are allies, the bond between us unbreakable. She would die for me, I know that, as I would for her.

"So come on then," she says, and I hear the smile in her voice.

"Maybe I should go back, get a torch," I say. I don't tell her that I find the cave eerie or that I'm afraid one of us might fall and get hurt, perhaps even tumble down an unseen chasm. Before she can comment I continue hurriedly, "I mean, what's the point of exploring if we can't see anything?"

She sighs deeply and the echoes remind me of the wind whispering in the trees last night. They make it sound as if we are not alone in the cave, as if there are others here with us, just out of sight.

"If you go back and Dad sees you he'll probably give you a job to do."

"He won't see me," I tell her. "I'll sneak in and sneak out again."

She is silent for a moment and then she says, "All right, but hurry up. I'll wait here."

Her shape blurs and shrinks, as if she is melting into the floor, but she is only sitting down.

I turn back to face the entrance, a jagged, vertical crack, like a lightning bolt, white with sunshine. Although I feel a lurch of alarm at the base of my throat, I tell myself that the entrance isn't *really* narrower than it was when we entered the cave. Even so, I try to hurry without making it obvious. Sunlight bleeds through the crack as I get closer, partially blinding me, blurring the definition of my surroundings. Unable to see properly, I miss my footing and my ankle turns on the uneven ground. Pain shoots up my leg and I gasp, stumbling sideways. As I raise my hands to stop my face from hitting the wall, Angie calls out, "Are you okay?"

The pain is like a firework, a burst of light followed by a slow ebb. "Fine," I say, placing my foot flat on the ground and tentatively putting my weight on it. "I just slipped."

"Be careful," Angie says.

I bark a quick laugh. "I don't think these caves like me."

"Course they do, they're friendly caves," she says, her voice hollow. "I feel as though they're hugging me. They make me feel safe."

I imagine vast, misshapen arms of rock closing around me, and shudder. As if afraid that the caves are somehow aware of my unease I hurry towards the entrance, the crack like a stretched-out Z, and push my way into the sunshine. At first the glare blinds me, but when I raise a hand to shield my eyes my vision is flooded with green. I hear a ripple and see my Dad sitting on the sloping lawn, facing away from the house, his back to me. The ripple is the sound of his newspaper as he turns the page. His hands are big and chunky, the backs hairy as the paws of an ape. Sometimes when he comes home from work, his hands are caked with plaster dust and look as if they're made of stone.

I creep behind him and into the house. I imagine him turning and seeing me; in my mind I rehearse how I will respond if he accuses me of deliberately trying to avoid him. How surprised should I look without overdoing it? How casual should I sound when I say, 'Oh, hi, Dad, I didn't see you there'? But he doesn't turn and within minutes I am slipping back into the cave with a heavy torch coated in black rubber, which I knew was sitting on a shelf in the kitchen cupboard because Mum used it to descend the steps last night when she went to fetch the Scrabble from the car.

As soon as I'm inside the cave I push the rubber-coated button with my thumb and a beam of light leaps across the rocky wall. Something in the rough grey stone glitters when the light hits it, though by contrast the surfaces that slant away from the light become so dark with shadow that it looks as though they're painted black. In fact, the torchlight makes the cave seem unreal, like a painting or a film set. I tilt the beam downwards, directing it at the ground, illuminating my way.

"I'm back," I call, though not too loudly in case Dad hears me.

Even though my voice is low, soft echoes, like the cooing of birds, tumble ahead of me. When there is no response I raise the torch, the light fanning out ahead. It doesn't quite reach the flat stone ridge on the gradual upwards slope of the path where Angie squatted down to wait. I move forward, the light slithering in front of me.

"Angie," I call. "Are you there?"

The light reaches the ridge and sidles across it, then up the wall beside it.

The ridge is unoccupied. Angie has gone.

I assure myself that it's nothing to worry about, that she just got tired of waiting; she has always been more impatient than me. I stride forward, the torch beam highlighting potential pitfalls. As the entrance dwindles behind me, I raise my voice. "Angie? Where are you?"

I reach the ridge and step up on to it, which causes the torchlight to jerk upwards. Looking beyond the ridge I feel a giddy sense of vertigo, because after this point the floor tumbles steeply away into darkness.

Or so it seems at first, as the light, still at head-height, skitters across the wall. When I point it downwards, however, half-expecting it to sink and fade into a black chasm, the rubble-covered floor beyond the ridge springs up at me.

The floor slopes downwards, though not steeply enough to be treacherous. I call again, a note of irritation in my voice, which the echoes turn sharp and wheedling. Again there is no reply. I pause to rub my ankle, which, though sore, does not particularly hamper me. Then I step down off the ridge onto the path beyond, moving deeper into the cave.

Where is Angie? Is she hiding from me? Has she moved so far ahead that she is out of earshot? But without a torch, surely the cave is pitch-black? I wonder how far back into the rock the cave goes, whether it will eventually branch out into a series of tunnels that become a maze. Is it possible to get lost in here? Perhaps I should have brought a piece of chalk to mark my way. I scan the floor, shifting chunks of stone with the toe of my trainer until I find one that I think is suitable. Picking it up I try it out on the wall, using it to scratch an X into the rock.

Ahead of me something shifts in the darkness.

I jerk the torch up and round, which gives the impression that the walls of the cave are wavering, flapping, like a canvas tent in a high wind. Shadows move ahead, and for an instant I have an impression of hunched shapes flooding from the darkness, of darting, insect-like movement. Even as the thought enters my head I know it to be false. It is nothing but my imagination that makes me feel I am being watched. Nevertheless my voice is a little ragged as I call my sister's name once again. Even before the echoes die, the cave around me fills with whispers.

I swing this way and that, half-expecting the torchlight to illuminate faces in the rock, pick out figures emerging from the shadows. But within seconds the swell of whispering voices dissipates and I realize once again that what I'm hearing are mostly echoes, and that the voices are only one voice, not many. I realize too that the whispering was not really whispering at all, but someone — Angie? — hushing me. I open my mouth to speak her name, then think better of it and creep forward, unraveling the darkness with torchlight, picking the shadows apart.

But still there is no sign of Angie. And then I see a black scar in the rock wall to my left. It is only as I get closer that I see it is a side tunnel, a narrow opening in the rock. I shine the torch into it, light flooding the space like water. The tunnel cuts straight through the rock for twenty metres before curving round to the right. At the bend where it does so, half out of sight, I make out the back of a crouching figure.

I step into the tunnel, torch held before me like a sword with which to defend myself. The figure remains motionless.

"Angie?" I whisper.

The figure half-turns its head and I see with relief that it is indeed my sister. She seems distracted. Her forehead wrinkles in a slight frown and she half-flaps a hand at me, urging me either to be quiet or to switch off the torch. Although I decide to say nothing more until I'm squatting beside her, I'm reluctant to plunge us into darkness, and so compromise by pointing the torch directly at the ground, reducing its field of influence. Instantly the cave fills with shadows, which seem to seep from the walls like ink through blotting paper. Angie is reduced to a lump of darkness; she is so still she could be mistaken for a marker stone. I edge towards her, light pooling around my shoes. It is only when I reach her and crouch beside her that I look beyond where she is squatting, and gasp.

I don't need the torchlight to tell me that the passage opens out ahead of us. Even in the darkness I sense the expansion of space; from the left comes a chill breeze that smells of earth and rock and cold water. For the second time in as many days I get the feeling that we have moved into another world, and I am gripped by a sudden image, or sensation, of infinite worlds, one tucked inside the other, each more mysterious than the last. I shift closer to Angie, the soles of my shoes scraping on rock, until our forearms are touching. The contact doesn't provide much comfort, however. Her skin is as cold as the stone wall.

"Are you okay?" I breathe into her ear.

She remains motionless. Even her head doesn't move. But she says, "It's so beautiful here, so serene. I don't want to go back."

That word, 'serene'. It sounds strange coming from her lips. I know what it means, but it is a word neither of us would ordinarily use. It is as though she has been challenged to use the word in conversation, or as if someone is speaking through her. However it is her last sentence that alarms me, though I decide to make light of it.

"Not sure Mum would be happy about that."

As soon as I say it I think: What about Dad? What would *he* say? Would he care if he never saw Angie again? Then I think: Who would he be most upset about losing? Angie or me?

Angie doesn't respond to my comment. She continues to stare into the darkness. I'm a bit spooked by her behaviour. My sister is normally the silly, energetic one, whereas I'm less spontaneous, more studious.

Jabbing her in the arm I say, "I wouldn't be happy either. I'd miss you."

A little dreamily she says, "You'd know where I was. You could visit me."

"It wouldn't be the same," I say. "Besides what would you eat? And how would you see anything? It's pitch black in here." I demonstrate by pressing my thumb on the rubber-coated button of the torch.

I've never known total darkness before. I feel vacuum-sealed by it, like a piece of fish you buy in the supermarket. I know that lack of light doesn't automatically mean lack of air, but I feel breathless all the same. I turn the torch back on again and look at Angie. Her eyes are wide and shining.

"I'd be provided for," she says.

"By who?"

As if I haven't spoken she continues, "And my eyes would change. The rest of me would change. I'd become like the night people."

I shiver, but tell myself it is only the breeze that raises goose bumps on my skin. "Who are the night people?"

"The people who live here. The Albion Fay. That's who the house is named after."

"People you've made up, you mean?" I say, the words coming out tetchily because I'm more nervous than I care to admit.

She turns and I only know she is smiling because the shadows around her mouth change shape.

From somewhere in the cavern ahead of us comes a sound. My guts clench icily. I give a thin, high gasp as I suck air too quickly into my lungs, and at the same moment I flip up the torch, directing it into the darkness. Light springs forward, then seems to drift slowly down as it dwindles into a soft radiance. I gasp again, exhaling this time. The cavern is vaster than I had anticipated, expanding upwards and outwards in all directions. It is a natural chamber, roughly spherical in shape, though the walls are by no means regular. There are juts and crags and ledges, and the rock face on the far side of the narrow valley, along the bottom of which gleams a black scar of water, is pocked and slashed with caves.

The sound I heard was a shifting of stones, a trickle of rubble, and indeed the torchlight picks out a minute landslide of dusty rock an instant before it comes to a halt. I tilt the torch so that the beam, weakened by distance, crawls higher, up to the dark slit from which the rockfall came. I see nothing, but I imagine something — an animal, a person — coming to the mouth of the cave, dislodging the rocks with its foot, then darting back in again. A shiver runs through me. I feel watched, vulnerable. I feel as though the torch is a beacon, exposing our position, but I don't want to switch it off. I would feel even worse in the darkness.

"Let's go," I say, reaching down to take Angie's cold, small hand in mine.

I expect her to argue, to say that we came here to explore, that we just got here, that we've got all morning.

I'm relieved, therefore, when she says, "Okay. The night people have gone now anyway. They don't like you."

I feel a little hurt. 'Well, I don't like them either,' I want to snap, but I don't. Instead I give her hand another tug and rise to my feet, pulling her with me.

"Come on."

Whenever I walk into the big Georgian house with its institutionalized smell of disinfectant over mildew and old carpets, my spirits sink. Nevertheless I force a smile as the girl behind the Reception desk, whose name I think is Natalie, says, "Good morning, Mr Ryan. How are you today?"

"Fine, thanks," I say.

Natalie grins as if that's the best news she's ever heard. "Patricia is so looking forward to your visit."

No one ever called my mother Patricia. It was always Pat. However I decide not to point this out. "Is she?" I say, unable to prevent a note of surprise from creeping into my voice.

"Absolutely," Natalie says, with such conviction that it looks as though she's determined to make herself believe it.

I want to ask how she can tell, but I'm not a confrontational person. Getting angry takes up too much energy and Natalie is only doing her job. It must be hard to stay upbeat in a place like this and I'm sure some of the visitors appreciate it. So instead I say, "Well, that's good." Then I gesture vaguely towards the swing door into the next corridor. "Where is she? Usual place?"

Natalie nods. "Yes, she's in the Day Room. Enjoying the sunshine."

Even though it is late November, harsh white sunlight blazes through the large windows which make up almost one entire wall of the Day Room. Despite this it is a cheerless place, the floor carpeted in thin, grey matting, the bare walls painted an insipid yellow that reminds me of school custard. The furniture, mostly comprising a haphazard scattering of wooden-framed armchairs with faux leather seats, looks old and tired, though not as old and tired as the armchairs' occupants. Most of them sit motionless, staring silently into space. Some twitch, or drool, or make guttural, animal-like sounds. One old lady, whose skin and hair seems composed of white dust, nods and pats the air and says, "There there... There there..." over and over again.

There are carers sitting with some of the old people — mostly women, but some men — who look up and beam at me as I pass among them. Some of the carers talk softly with their charges or attempt to play board games or do jigsaws with them. I see Mum sitting with a crocheted blanket over her knees, staring out of the window. She looks so frail that the sunlight seems to be eating her away, reducing her slowly to stardust.

As always I find it difficult to equate this pitiful scrap of humanity with the robust, intelligent, resourceful woman she once was. The Alzheimer's has aged her prematurely. She is only seventy-one, but she looks ninety. I have always thought her condition a curse, but now, in light of what has happened, perhaps it is a blessing. I walk over and sit down on the wooden chair that has been placed there in anticipation of my arrival. Leaning towards her, I say, "Hello, Mum."

Though she turns to look at me her eyes are unfocused. It is as though she is looking through me, at the wall.

"Hello there, Chris. Is our Angie not with you?"

I try not to wince. "It's not Chris, Mum. It's Frank. Your son."

I take her hand, as if in the hope that physical contact with her own flesh and blood will jog her memory, help clear her mind, but she looks alarmed, and so I let her hand go.

"Is our Angie still at school?" she asks.

I see panic in her eyes as she struggles to master her thoughts, or perhaps I only imagine that I do.

I decide not to complicate matters by trying to explain. Instead I repeat firmly, "It's Frank, Mum. Your son. You remember me, don't you?"

I peer into her eyes, willing them to clear. This is the woman who once put down the word 'diptych' in Scrabble and explained to Angie and I exactly what it meant; this is the woman who, in her twenties and thirties, defied our father's contempt by working her way ravenously and gleefully through the novels of Thomas Hardy, Jane Austen, Wilkie Collins, D.H. Lawrence and the Bronte sisters.

She stares back at me now and all I see is blankness and confusion. Finally, tentatively, she says, "Remind me again what school you go to, dear. Are you in my grand-daughter's class?"

My throat aches with grief and frustration. My thoughts feel heavy and dull, as if the illness that has devoured the memories of so many in this room is now beginning to affect me as well.

"I'm Frank, Mum," I say again. "I'm forty-eight years old. I was born in 1965. You gave birth to me. Don't you remember?"

"In the hospital?" she offers helpfully.

"Yes," I say. "In the hospital."

"Is that where I am now," she asks, looking around. "Have you come to visit me? When can I go home?"

I try not to sigh. I don't want her to think she's upset or disappointed me. "Soon, Mum," I say, knowing that a minute from now she won't remember. "You can go home soon."

"To Albion Fay?" she asks, and I blink in surprise.

"What did you say?"

"Angie turned her clothes inside-out, do you remember?"

"Yes," I whisper, staring at her, "I do."

Then she laughs and for a moment she sounds young again, she sounds like the mother I remember.

"Of course you don't," she says. "I know you're only being kind. You and Angie didn't meet until much later, did you, Chris?"

Despair surges in me. Anger too. *It's Frank!* I want to shout. *I'm Frank! Not Chris! Frank!*

But instead I simply shake my head. "No," I say, the anger ebbing, leaving me nothing but weary. "No, we didn't."

This time she reaches out and takes *my* hand and pats it. Her eyes are kindly. "Thank you for coming to see me, Chris. You're like a son to me. Do you know that?"

"Yes," I say.

She releases my hand, then settles back in her chair and looks out of the window. The sun falls on her face, and although it obliterates her wrinkles it also bleaches the colour from her eyes.

*

When I enter the pub I see that Angie's sitting with someone. She half-stands up and waves me over. She looks almost eager.

As I raise a hand in response and walk over to her table I try to smile, to hide the concern that I feel. Angie looks thin and washed-out and older than her twenty-three years. Around her eyes her skin looks dark, almost bruised, and her hair, pulled into a loose ponytail, is flat and lank. Even her clothes look tired, her blouse wrinkled, her faded jeans barely clinging to her bony hips. As I get closer I notice that the fingernails of her right hand, which is curled around a half-pint of cider, are bitten to the quick.

This is the first time I've seen my sister for three, maybe four months. I ring her at least once a week — though she never rings me — to see how she is, but whenever I suggest getting together she always puts me off. I've never been to her basement flat, which I know is in a shabby area of the city, an area inhabited largely by students and the unemployed and itinerant workers. She has been to my house twice, but mostly when I see her, which is rarely, it is at Mum's, where we congregate for Christmases and birthdays.

I know that Mum worries about Angie, and is disappointed with how she has turned out, though she never actually says as much. What she does say is that Angie was always 'such a bright young thing' and that if she applied herself she could do so much better. I know that Angie has had a variety of jobs since leaving school. She has worked in restaurants and cafes and takeaways, and in the box office of a theatre, and as a cleaner in a leisure centre. But when it comes to employment she is like a butterfly, fluttering from one job to another, never settling in one place for long. I don't know whether she gets bored and leaves, or whether, more often than not, she gets the sack for being unreliable, for taking too much time off. Her psychiatric history can't help, the fact that she has spent the past dozen years or so on various types of medication, and in and out of hospitals and institutions. As far as I'm aware she is currently working in a charity shop, though whether this is paid work or whether she is merely there on a voluntary basis I have no idea.

I was surprised when she called me yesterday and invited me out to the pub. Surprised and suspicious.

"Are you all right?" I asked her.

She laughed, and although she has spent much of the past twelve years *not* being all right, she told me that of course she was.

"What's this in aid of then?" I said.

She sounded almost playful, almost like the sister I had once known. "Do I have to have a reason to ask my own brother out for a drink?"

I wondered whether she was in trouble, whether she needed money. I said, "It's a bit unexpected, that's all."

There was a pause, and I wondered if she was reflecting on how distant she had been over the past few years. Finally she said, "There's something I want to tell you."

As I reach the table now Angie surprises me by standing up and giving me a fierce hug. I hug her back and am alarmed by the fact that she feels even thinner and frailer than she looks. She clutches me tightly, and a little too long, as if she wishes to convey her gratitude for not giving up on her. Finally she releases me and I see that her sallow face has gained a little colour, twin spots of red on her sharp cheekbones, which quickly fade.

She turns to the man sitting quietly at the table behind her and says, "Frank, this is Chris."

The man, Chris, extends a hand towards me. He has shaggy hair and a sparse moustache and narrow-framed glasses with a dark tint to them. He wears a chunky blue-grey jumper that smells sweetly of marijuana smoke, and on the table before him is a battered tobacco tin, on top of which rest half a dozen thin roll-ups.

"Hello," I say.

"Nice to meet you, mate." He has a North Eastern accent. "Angie talks about you all the time."

"Does she?" I say, unable to prevent myself from sounding surprised.

He grins. "Sometimes I think I know you better than I know her."

I go to the bar for drinks. Chris has a pint of Guinness and Angie has another half a cider, but I only have a Coke because I'm driving. When I get back to the table they're both smoking roll-ups, their shoulders touching as though they're propping one another up. In my shirt and jacket and university scarf, my hair neatly trimmed, I feel stuffy and conventional, and also oddly unsettled. Then I realize that what *makes* me unsettled is the fact that for the first time in my sister's company I feel like the outsider. Angie has had boyfriends before — though not many — but it's always previously been the other guy who's been the gooseberry when the three of us have been together. Not intentionally so; it's just the way it's been, the natural order of things. In truth, nothing has *ever* been quite the same since Albion Fay, but if there *is* one person that Angie has been able to maintain any kind of connection with, it's me.

This, though, is new. Purely by her body language I sense she's given more of herself to Chris than she's ever given to anyone else. Am I jealous? Happy for my sister? Fearful for her? I think, if I'm honest, I feel all of those things. But I try to be nothing but friendly. I smile and sip my drink.

"So what do you do, Chris?" I ask, and immediately think: Boring question. Boring and perhaps competitive. Am I asking because I'm genuinely interested? Because I want to know whether he is a suitable partner for my sister? Or simply because I'm eager to learn whether I've got a 'better' job than he has?

It turns out Chris is the manager not only of the shop that Angie works in, but of all the shops that the charity owns in the area. He has a degree in Physics from Liverpool University, he likes cycling and mountaineering, and he supports Newcastle United. His mum still lives in Newcastle, in the house where Chris was born, but his dad died of cancer nine years ago, when Chris was sixteen. He has two older sisters, one a solicitor in London and the other the wife of a South African businessman. He and Angie have been a couple for eight months, and for the past month they have been living together in Chris's house on the outskirts of the city.

"So it's serious then?" I say, keeping my voice light.

Angie looks suddenly coy. She reaches for Chris's hand and they mesh fingers. "It's more than that," she says. "We wanted you to be the first to know."

I guess what she's going to say before she says it, but I prepare myself to look happy and surprised.

"We're getting married," she tells me.

*

In the two days since Angie and I entered the cave, Angie has been quiet and subdued, which is not like her at all. Yesterday we spent the day at the beach, and although the two of us built a sand castle and splashed in the sea and spent hours pottering in rock pools, looking for crabs — partly to get away from our bickering parents — I couldn't help feeling that she was with me in body only, that her thoughts were elsewhere.

This morning, over breakfast, I suggest that we head towards the tall chimney in the woods that we can see sticking up above the trees like a giant periscope. When I propose the idea, Angie says, "What about the caves?"

"We've already been in the caves," I say.

"We've been in *one*," she replies. "There's loads more to explore."

"But they're cold and dark and I want to be out in the sunshine," I insist.

"Quite right too," Mum says from the sink, where she's standing with pink Marigold gloves on, washing the breakfast dishes.

Angie scowls, an expression which only deepens when Mum says, "You should make the most of this nice weather. It's not often you get the chance to be outside in this country."

"But the caves are *interesting*, Mum," Angie says.

"And I'm sure they'll be just as interesting on another day when the weather's not so nice," Mum says.

Feeling a need to convince my sister, I say encouragingly, "It'll be fun, Angie."

She glares at me. "No it won't, it'll be stupid."

"Not as stupid as poking about in the dark and looking at a load of old rocks," I retort before I can help myself.

"For God's sake!" Mum snaps, swinging round so violently that an arc of soapy bubbles flies from the washing-up brush she's holding and spatters on the floor. "Don't *you* two start arguing! I have enough of that with-" She cuts herself off abruptly, but a glance at the ceiling leaves us in no doubt that she's talking about Dad, who, after bad-temperedly scoffing his bacon and eggs, is now upstairs having a shower.

Recovering her composure, Mum says, "Just remember that we're here for a whole week, so you'll have plenty of time to explore the caves *and* the woods before we go home. So let's have no more bickering, all right?"

She looks at Angie, who shrugs and sullenly says, "All right."

By 9:30am we're ready. I have a backpack full of drinks and snacks, which Mum has provided for us, even though we've promised that we'll be back for lunch at 12:30. As we prepare to set off, Dad comes into the kitchen, his hair still wet from the shower. He sees the backpack and says, "Where are you two off to?"

I tense, thinking that he'll prevent us from going for no reason other than to spoil our fun. "Exploring," I say.

He laughs. "Oh, aye. Sure you're up to that? What if you see a squirrel or a rabbit? Sure you won't get frightened?"

"Don't tease them, George," Mum says quickly. "They're just going for a walk in the woods. It'll do them good, nice bit of fresh air."

Dad grunts and shoots me a look of such contempt that I feel a pulse start to hammer in my throat. Face burning, I glance down at the strap of my rucksack and pretend to adjust it.

I imagine Dad's eyes burning into the top of my head, but then he says, "I'm off to get a paper. Have a lovely time, ladies."

He stomps out. Mum says something under her breath, but then abruptly switches on a smile. "Right, you two, all set?"

The three of us don't usually mention Dad's moods, I guess because if we ignore them we can pretend they don't exist. Now, though, Angie asks deliberately, "What's wrong with Dad?"

Mum gives her a sharp look, then smiles bitterly. "Oh, he's just mardy because he's not getting what he wants."

"What's that?" Angie asks bluntly.

Another look from Mum, longer and more calculating this time. I feel as if there's more to the exchange than meets the eye, but I can't work out what it is.

"It's something he doesn't deserve," Mum says, in a way that makes it clear that's all she will say on the matter.

Angie and I walk down the steps that wind through the garden and through the gate at the bottom. Then we cross the dirt road, looking both ways even though we haven't seen any car except our own on this road since we got here. I'm surprised to find that beyond the screen of trees and bushes on the far edge of the road the ground slopes steeply downwards. It's so steep that you have to lean back to stop your legs from running away with you.

We don't say anything at first. We just lunge down the slope side by side. Sunlight falls through the gaps in the canopy of leaves overhead like confetti made of light. We hear birds singing and bees going zzzzz, which reminds me of the sound people make in The Beano when they're asleep. I say this to Angie and she laughs. Then she says, "Sorry for being mardy."

I shrug without looking at her, focusing on where I'm putting my feet. "That's all right."

At the bottom of the slope we stop and look around. The ground levels out here, but the trees become thicker. Even so there's what looks like a path that winds through them, though it's overgrown with ferns and nettles that make me wish I'd worn jeans and not shorts.

"How come you're so mad on the caves anyway?" I ask. I glance at Angie to see the expression on her face before she speaks, but the sun gets in my eyes and all I see is an orangey-brown blur.

I tilt my head until leaves block out the sun and her features swim into view, but her expression is so bland that I feel she's already covered up what she's thinking. I feel uncomfortable again, and a bit sad. Angie and I have never kept secrets from one another.

Now, though, it's as if a window which has always been clear has suddenly become scratched and cloudy. I wonder what happened in the caves. I know it's silly, but I can't help thinking of that film, *The Exorcist*, that caused a big fuss a couple of years ago. In it a girl gets the devil inside her, and at first she's normal, but then she starts to change, as if the devil is pushing its way out through her skin. I haven't seen it, but Mum and Dad have, and Mum told me all about it. Dad said it was a load of rubbish, but Mum said it was the scariest film she'd ever seen.

Angie looks normal, but I know there's something different about her. She shrugs and says, "They're mysterious. And they make me happy. I feel safe when I'm in them."

"Even though it's dark?" I ask.

"*Because* it's dark. No one can find me in the caves if I don't want them to."

"Not even the night people?"

As she reaches up to push sweaty strands of hair out of her face, I can't help thinking that what she's really doing is hiding her eyes, as though there's something in them that she doesn't want me to see.

"The night people belong there," she says. "They won't hurt you if you don't hurt them. They don't want to draw attention to themselves."

They're not real, though, are they? I want to say, but I can't get the words out. I'm afraid of what her answer will be.

Instead I turn away and point at the overgrown path through the trees. "I think if we go that way," I say, "we'll eventually come to the chimney."

Angie suddenly grins and darts ahead. "Come on then," she cries. "Last one there is a fat pig!"

"Hey!" I shout. "Not fair!" But I feel a lightness in my heart as I go after her. This is the Angie I know, the Angie that's been missing these past two days. I roar like a bear, and she screams, and I laugh, and I try to ignore the suspicion that she's only pretending to be like her old self to distract me from asking more questions about the night people.

We haven't run far before a nettle slashes my shin and makes me hop in pain. Even though all you can see is a little red stripe on the skin of my leg, it feels as if my flesh is burning. As I grit my teeth and sit on the ground, scratching at the sting, Angie looks for some dock leaves. She finds some, rips them out at the roots and rubs them vigorously on my leg, covering the red patch in cool green sap.

When the stinging subsides I climb to my feet and adjust the rucksack, which is making my back sweaty, and we proceed more slowly than before, wary of craning clumps of nettles. I find a stick and use it like a machete, hacking foliage out of our way. The track, which is less like a path and more like a vague darkish stripe bisecting the thick undergrowth, as if someone has only recently forced their way through the woods ahead of us, seems to weave aimlessly and I become anxious that we might get lost.

"Maybe we should have brought a compass," I say, coming to a halt and looking around.

Angie shakes her head and flaps a hand in the direction we're going. "Don't need one. This is the right way."

"How do you know?"

She gives a slow blink, as if the sun is making her drowsy. "I just do."

I'm about to argue when I hear a brief thrashing of undergrowth followed by a stifled gasp or giggle.

It comes from somewhere to our left, though it's difficult to tell from how far away. I stop dead and glance back at Angie. It's clear that she has heard the sound too.

There's nothing to see, though, except trees and bushes, filled with nodding green shadows and twinkling coins of sunlight.

"Who's there?" I shout. I want my words to ring out in the still air, but my voice sounds thin and frightened, which makes me cringe. I try again, trying to make my voice deeper and rougher this time. "We know you're there. There's no use hiding."

My words die away, leaving a silence that is all at once so deep that I imagine every woodland creature — every fox, rabbit, squirrel, bird, mouse — suddenly becoming still, ears pricked to listen.

After a few seconds Angie says, "Must have been an animal. Let's carry on."

We do, but now I feel nervous. From everywhere around me I sense movement. My head darts left and right, but all I see are gently waving leaves and changing angles of light and shadow as the canopy shifts overhead.

Twice more I halt and raise a hand, certain I can hear rustling close by. Whenever Angie and I stop, though, the sounds stop too.

"It's just the wind," Angie says.

Or the night people I almost respond, but I know that if I speak the words they won't sound like the joke I mean them to be and so I stay silent.

After another couple of minutes the landscape ahead of us changes. First Angie spots what looks like bits of red-brick buildings through the tangle of tree trunks and branches, and then the trees and bushes peter out, like an army which has been forced to halt at the edge of a precipice.

Angie and I halt too, though not because we can't carry on. We do it in order to take in the scene before us.

In a huge, bowl-like hollow below are the ruins of what looks like some kind of smelting works or factory. There are walls everywhere, though no roofs; it is like looking down into a massive red-brick maze. Some of the walls are intact and almost as tall as the trees around them; others are nothing but jagged remains, jutting out of the earth like old, broken teeth. Metal girders, which must once have supported floors that have long since collapsed, form makeshift bridges from one wall to another or lean within the chasms between them. Lower down, beneath ground level, cell-like alcoves made out of moss-covered slabs of grey stone have been exposed, inside which are crumbling, hive-like structures, each about the size of a small cottage, which Angie and I think might once have been kilns or ovens. Stretching between these walls, on a number of different levels, are half-collapsed staircases choked with weeds and rubble, and running alongside the ruin, on the far side, are a set of tracks, half-hidden by undergrowth, for what must once have been trains that carried goods to and from the factory through the woods.

Striking though all of this is, however, what really catches our eye is the chimney. Dominating everything around it, it rises high above the canopy of trees, pointing towards Heaven like the finger of God.

For maybe twenty seconds neither of us says anything, and then Angie turns to me with shining eyes. "Brill," she breathes.

I know what she's thinking and it makes me nervous. Sure enough she says, "Let's explore."

I look at some of the taller walls, many of which are cracked and leaning. "It looks a bit dangerous."

"It'll be fine," she says dismissively. "It's probably been here for ages. It's not just suddenly going to collapse, is it?"

Why not? I want to say. *Some of it's already collapsed.* But even

I'm getting bored of how cautious and anxious I'm being. So instead I say, "All right. But let's be careful."

She rolls her eyes and crosses to a flight of 'steps', which are nothing but a series of gouges hacked from the sloping earth. As we descend, arms held out for balance like trapeze artists, I feel as if the ground is rising around us, squeezing the sky smaller. Down below it feels cooler, as if a chill is seeping from the ruins. We pick our way across crumbling bricks that lie everywhere, peppering the ground.

Although it hasn't rained for days the vegetation down here looks limp and bedraggled. Clots of mossy fungus grow on tree trunks and mouldering brickwork; sagging branches drip with clumps of slimy green weed or algae that looks like witch's hair. A damp, mulchy odour clings to everything, so pungent I feel as if it's lining the back of my throat every time I breathe in.

I look up at some of the less stable-looking walls, wondering whether the vibrations of our footsteps will be enough to make them topple. Angie, though, doesn't seem worried. She ducks through a rotted wooden doorway whose lintel has snapped in the middle, forming a V, and picks her way carefully over mounds of rubble and decomposing vegetation until she's standing in the middle of what looks like a tall, square tower without a roof.

She spreads her arms wide, tilts her head back to peer at the sky, and lets out a whoop. The sound echoes up and up; I imagine it ricocheting like a bullet from wall to wall. Just before the echo dies away, I hear what sounds like a giggle from above and once again I feel sure that someone is watching us.

"Listen," I hiss, looking through the doorway at Angie, who is still standing with her arms spread and her head back, as if offering herself as a sacrifice.

As if it's a big effort she lets her head fall forward and opens her eyes. She looks at me, but her face is so blank that for a second it's as though whatever she offered has been taken, as though the essence of her has been snatched away. Then she blinks. "What?"

"Didn't you hear it?"

"Hear what? I only heard myself."

I take a few steps forward until I'm standing on the threshold of the doorway, but I don't go through. Lowering my voice I say, "Someone laughed."

She sighs, as if I'm being tiresome. "Who?"

"Well, I don't know, do I?" Glancing around I murmur, "I think someone else is here."

Instead of keeping our suspicions between us she looks up and shouts, "If there are any peeping toms out there, show yourselves." When there's no response she grins at me. "Maybe I should give them something to look at."

"What do you mean?"

Again she spreads her arms and spins around. "Don't you just love all this nature? Doesn't it make you feel free and wild?"

I shrug.

Frowning she raises her voice. "Doesn't it just make you want to take all your clothes off and dance naked?"

There is a hiss of excitement or anticipation from somewhere above us, or so I imagine. Alarmed I shake my head. "No."

Angie's grin is manic now. Her eyes glitter. "Is that what you want, you perverts?" she shouts suddenly. "Shall I take all my clothes off and dance for you?"

There is no response for a moment and then I see movement. It's above us, on the rim of the hollow. I see a shape rise up that I assume is a figure, but because light from the sun-drenched sky is pouring through the trees behind it, I can't be sure. It looks about the right shape for a figure, but it's black and featureless, its outline shimmering. I raise a hand to shield my eyes, and as I do so a second shape rises up from the rim of the hollow, about twenty yards from the first, and then a third. Realizing that Angie and I are outnumbered I feel a pang of fear.

For a moment the figures stand, staring down at us — or at least that's what I imagine they're doing. I glance at Angie. She's shielding her eyes with her hand now too, though I don't see fear on her face, only curiosity. Despite myself I think about the night people, the Fay. What if they're real? What if they've crept out from the caves and followed us?

Then the first of the figures to rise, who still looks like nothing but a wavering black stump despite my attempt to blot out the sun, calls out, "Go on then."

I wonder what he means and then I remember the last thing that Angie said. She snorts loudly. "You wish."

Although she's small and skinny and not very strong, she doesn't look scared. I try not to look scared too, even though my guts are quaking so hard I feel it's only a matter of time before it spreads to my limbs.

The figure above us laughs. It's not a nice sound.

"Who are you?" Angie shouts defiantly. "Why have you been following us?"

Something seems to break away from one of the figures, a dark chunk of itself, and then I realize it's a rock, about the size of a fist. It hits the ground half-way down the slope and bounces, spinning in the air, gaining speed and momentum as it hurtles in our direction.

I flinch and duck, raising my hands to protect my head, but

Angie stands her ground, hands on hips, watching the progress of the rock as it hits a metal girder somewhere above us with a clang and bounces off into the trees.

"Hey!" I shout, my voice, high-pitched, wavering. "Watch it!"

The figures above cackle and whoop with laughter. They remind me of baboons.

"That was clever," Angie taunts them. "Is that how you get your kicks? From throwing rocks like cavemen?"

There is silence, then one of the figures, the last to rise, says, "Who are you anyway?"

"None of your business," Angie says.

"We can *make* it our business," another of the figures replies. I've heard enough now to guess that the dark shapes are all older kids, maybe fourteen or fifteen.

"Why don't you then?" Angie challenges them.

"All right, we will."

The three figures seem to shrink, but only because they're starting to move down the slope towards us. Angie watches them approach with interest, but my guts are juddering so hard that I can hear it in my voice as I hiss, "We should get out of here."

Angie looks defiant. "I'm not scared of them."

"We don't even know who they are."

"They don't know who *I* am. If they try anything I'll show them a few kung fu moves."

Sometimes her recklessness baffles me. It's like she doesn't care what happens to her, like she has no concept of danger or pain. As the boys approach I begin to see them more clearly. I'm not encouraged by their appearance. They look rough, like the kids from the council estate back home that I always try to avoid. The one who showed himself first, and who I think of as their leader, is the tallest. He has long, straggly, dirty-looking hair and despite the heat he wears a black bomber jacket over a tight red jumper with stars on it. The one who threw the rock is squat with a long fringe of black hair that he keeps flicking out of his eyes, and a face like a grumpy gorilla. The third is skinny with a crew cut, and he walks funny, like there's something wrong with his legs.

As they get closer I tense, clenching my fists to stop my hands from shaking. Angie, though, still doesn't look scared at all as she steps casually out of the sagging doorway and wanders over to stand beside me. Two against three, I think. Two ten year olds, one of them a girl, against three fifteen year old boys. I wonder what's going to happen. For once I wish I was more like Dad.

When the boys are almost at the bottom of the slope, Angie steps forward and points at the tall kid.

"I like your jacket," she says.

The tall kid looks surprised. He glances down at himself as if to check what he's wearing, and then he looks up. "Thanks," he mutters.

"Where did you get it from?"

He shrugs. "Market."

"Can I try it on?"

He looks confused, but says, "Yeah, all right."

Still looking as though he doesn't know what he's doing or why, he peels off his jacket and hands it over. Angie smiles as she takes it, and even though the tall kid has big sweat patches under his arms, she shrugs it on without hesitation. It swamps her, the sleeves coming down over her hands, but she struts about like a fashion model in front of the boys, tossing her head back, making them laugh.

"It's a brill jacket," she says, "I love it." And then almost in the same breath she asks, "What are your names?"

Two of the boys tell her without hesitation. The tall kid is called Gary and the skinny kid is Scott. The black-haired kid remains silent until Gary stares at him, and then, narrowing his eyes, he mutters, "Carl."

"What about you?" Gary asks.

"I'm Angie," Angie says, "and this is my brother, Frank."

"Don't say much, does he?" says Scott. He has an odd voice, shrill and nasal and a bit buzzy, like he's swallowed a bee.

"No, but he thinks a lot," Angie says. "He's smart."

"Clever boy, are yer?" says Carl. "Fucking swot?"

"No," I mutter.

"You look like a swot. What yer got in that fucking bag?"

"Nothing," I say, forcing the words through a throat that feels clogged. "Just some provisions."

Carl pulls an exaggerated hoity-toity sort of face. "Ooh, *provisions*. Caviar and cucumber sandwiches, is it?"

Angie nods at Carl, then grins at Gary. "Is he always like this?"

"Like what?" says Carl aggressively, but Gary laughs and nods. "Yeah, he's a fucking idiot."

"Fuck off," Carl snarls.

Ignoring him, Angie says, "So you lot all from round here?"

Carl glowers at her, but Gary and Scott nod.

"What's it like?" Angie asks.

"Fucking boring," says Gary.

"So you not from round here then?" says Scott.

"Nah," says Angie. "We're on holiday."

"Where you staying?" asks Scott.

Angie gestures vaguely upwards. "In a house up there. A place called Albion Fay."

A look passes between the boys. Even Carl snorts and raises his eyebrows. "Rather you than me," Scott says.

The way he says it makes me shiver, but Angie leans forward, her eyes dancing. "Why, what's wrong with it?"

Gary looks at her steadily. "Supposed to be haunted, isn't it?"

"Is it?" she says eagerly.

"Weird things happen there," says Scott.

Angie turns and stares at him and he blushes slightly. "Oh yeah? Like what?"

"There're stories," says Gary. "Want to hear 'em?"

I don't, but Angie nods. "Definitely. Are they to do with the caves?"

Scott looks so startled that it's almost funny. "What do you know about the caves?"

"Nothing," says Angie. "Only that I've been in them."

"I wouldn't go in 'em if you paid me," says Scott.

"Why not? We've both been in them, haven't we, Frank?" She looks at me and I nod. A slow smile crosses her face and her eyes gleam even more brightly. "I like them."

Carl has been mooching silently about on the periphery of the group, edging closer to me, kicking stones about. Now suddenly he darts forward, shoving me in the side of the head with one hand and yanking the rucksack off my back with the other.

"Let's have a look in here," he shouts. "Let's see what you've got."

"Hey!" I shout, but I make no move to stop him. He's small for a fifteen year old, but he's still bigger than me, and as solid as a bulldog. He sneers triumphantly and digs his fingers into the top of the rucksack, which look like wrinkled lips puckered for a kiss. As he yanks them apart, Angie shrugs, unconcerned.

"Go ahead," she says. "It's only crisps and pop and stuff. You can share them with us if you like. We can have a picnic while you tell us about Albion Fay."

She's smart, Angie. By offering the boys a share in our food it means that if Carl steals it or stamps on it or starts throwing it about he's messing up not only our treats, but Gary's and Scott's too. Mum would call it taking the wind out of Carl's sails, and that's just what it's like. He stands there looking deflated and a bit silly, with the open rucksack in his hand.

"Yeah, well, I was only messing about," he says, and he swings the rucksack back towards me on one of its straps. I catch it before it can hit me in the face. My ear is throbbing from where he swatted me with his meaty hand, but I don't let it show. Angie suggests sitting down and sharing out the food and the other boys comply, Carl reluctantly. Gary and Scott perch themselves on a buckled girder sticking out of the ground, I sit on a big grey stone that feels a bit damp and Angie squats on a heap of bricks, which shift slightly beneath her. Carl slumps against a nearby tree, his arms folded, scowling. I open the rucksack, feeling like Santa with his sack of toys, and start to dole out the food — bags of crisps and Milky Ways and bottles of fizzy orange and a packet of custard creams.

When we're all eating, Angie says, "So tell us about Albion Fay."

Gary looks at Scott, who says, "My gran says the caves behind the house are a gateway that lead down to the underworld."

Carl takes a swig of fizzy orange and belches loudly. "Your gran's a nutter."

Scott's ears turn red. "She is not!"

"Yeah she is. She got shell shock in the war and it made her go bonkers. Everyone says so."

Scott jumps up. "Come here and say that, you fucking bastard!"

Carl laughs nastily. "You'll be sorry if I do."

"Not as sorry as you'll be," says Scott.

Gary points at Carl. "Shut up or fuck off."

Carl glowers at him for a moment, but then huffs and sits down.

"Go on, Scott," says Angie gently.

Scott is still standing up, his face so red he looks like a giant matchstick. After a moment, though, the tension in his body eases and he sits down.

"Why does your gran think the caves lead to the underworld?" Angie asks.

Scott shrugs. "She just does. 'Cos of all the weird things that have happened there."

"Like what?" asks Angie.

"Strange figures have been seen in the caves and in the woods round here, especially at night."

"The night people," I say.

Everyone looks at me as if they'd forgotten I'm here. My face feels suddenly hot and I guess that I'm blushing. To deflect attention away from myself I say quickly, "They're what Angie calls the people she says live in the caves."

Gary frowns. "So you already know about them?"

Angie shakes her head. "No."

"So how come you call them the night people?"

"I told you, I've been in the caves," she says. "I just know they're there, that's all."

Gary and Scott look at Angie with something like admiration, or even awe, but she just says, "Carry on, Scott."

He bites into a custard cream, as if giving himself time to collect his thoughts, and then in a muffled voice interspersed with crunches he says, "Whoever they are, my gran says they're not like normal people. She says they get angry if you look at them. She also says they bite." He glances at Angie as if for confirmation, but she just continues to stare at him, before finally murmuring, "The Fay."

"What?" Gary says, frowning. "Like the house, you mean?"

Angie nods. "Our mum told us that fay was an old word for fairy. Didn't she, Frank?"

"Yeah," I say.

"Fairies," scoffs Carl. "*You're* all fucking fairies if you think they exist." He suddenly glances up and jabs a finger off into the trees. "Ooh, look, there's Tinkerbell."

Angie hardly moves. She reminds me of a teacher dealing with a naughty child by refusing to get cross or give it the attention it demands.

Finally she says, "I don't think that was the kind of fairy Scott was talking about — was it, Scott?"

Scott shakes his head. "My gran says real fairies are ancient, dangerous creatures. She'd throw a fit if she knew I was here. She doesn't like me coming to these woods."

"Why are they dangerous?" I ask, curiosity getting the better of my shyness. "What do they do?"

"They steal children away from their families," Scott says. "They take them and put changelings in their place."

"What's a changeling?" I ask.

"A sort of copy, I think. I don't know for definite, but I'm pretty sure it's something bad."

Vague though the explanation is, it conjures a curdling sense of dread inside me. I imagine some dark entity disguised as a child lurking at the heart of a family like a poisonous spider at the centre of a web.

"Why do they do that?" I ask.

Scott looks impatient. "They just do."

"Has it ever happened at Albion Fay?"

He shrugs. "I don't know. But a family disappeared once."

"When?" asks Angie.

"A long time ago, I think. Back in the war."

Carl snorts. "They probably just scarpered 'cos they couldn't pay the rent."

Scott shakes his head. "No, my gran says they left all their stuff behind. She says there were half-eaten meals on the table and stuff like that."

"Is that true?" I say.

"My gran says it is."

There is silence for a moment as we all absorb this, then Gary says, "Tell them about the dogs."

"What dogs?" Angie asks, leaning forward. Her eagerness unsettles me.

Scott pauses as if deliberately drawing out the tension. "My gran says the Fay or the night people or whatever they're called, have no real shape of their own, and so they take on the shapes of people or animals. She says there've been lots of stories of people seeing black dogs in these woods because that's one of the things they change into. There was this one time a few years ago where a woman was taking her dog for a walk when it was getting dark. She was walking along the path at the front of the house you're staying in when suddenly these three black dogs with red eyes appeared in front of her. The woman said the dogs didn't bark or growl, they just stood there like they wanted to stop her from going any further. She said it was weird because her own dog, which normally barked and wagged its tail when it saw other dogs, was so scared that it started shivering and wouldn't move and she had to pick it up. The woman was scared too, so she turned round and started to walk back the way she'd come, but the dogs followed her. They didn't run or anything, they just walked along behind her, and they were so silent that the only way she knew they were still there was because every time she looked back she could see their red eyes shining in the dark. Anyway, this went on for a bit with her walking along, looking forward, then back, then forward again, until one time she looked back and the dogs weren't there any more. They'd vanished into thin air."

His voice has grown hushed and his eyes are large and round. He pauses, as if for effect.

"Bollocks," says Carl.

"It's not bollocks," Scott says, scowling. "It's true. My gran told me."

"It's still bollocks," says Carl. "Even if it's true, the dogs probably belonged to someone else. They probably just got bored of following the woman and went off into the woods."

Scott shakes his head. "No, the woman says there wasn't time. She says she kept turning round every couple of seconds. She says one second they were there and the next they were gone."

Carl snorts. "She just imagined it 'cos she was on her own and it was getting dark."

Scott looks unhappy, but he says, "Yeah, but that's not the whole story."

"Why? What else happened?" asks Angie.

But Scott's sulking now. He looks at Carl. "He'll only make fun of me if I tell you."

Angie turns and looks at Carl. "Fuck him. And fuck what he thinks. I want to know how the story ends."

Her voice is so hard and cold, and the look she gives Carl so intense, that for a moment everyone is shocked. There's a silence, which even Carl looks too intimidated to break. And then Gary barks out a laugh.

"Nice one," he hoots and looks at Scott. "You'll *have* to tell her now."

Scott flashes a look at Carl and smiles thinly, as if he's won some sort of victory. Then he looks into Angie's eyes, as if he's directing what he says only to her.

"After she heard the story my gran looked for this woman and found her. The woman told her there was something she'd never told anyone else 'cos she was scared people would think she was barmy. She said that after the dogs disappeared it was quiet for a few seconds and then she heard laughing. She said it sounded like children, but it was way up high in the trees and after a few seconds it faded as if whoever was doing it was moving away really quickly."

I shiver, but Angie grins. "Then what happened?" she asks.

Scott shrugs. "Nothing, except that the woman ran like hell. She ran all the way back to her car, which was like a mile away or something, carrying her dog. She told my gran she'd never been so terrified in her life and couldn't stop shaking for hours afterwards. She says the sound of that laughing up in the trees was the worst thing she'd ever heard."

*

The next afternoon we're supposed to go to a castle, but Mum and Dad have a big row over lunch and Dad storms out and drives away in the car. Mum goes upstairs, looking angry and upset, and Angie goes after her.

Left alone, feeling hollow and sick, I decide to read my book in the garden. As I step out into the sunshine I remember what Angie said yesterday about how she feels safe in the caves, and how no one would be able to find her in them if she didn't want them to. I wish I had somewhere to go where no one could find me, somewhere I could be on my own for a while, away from my fractured family. I look over at the caves, which resemble gaping mouths and hollow eyes, black against the grey rock, and I imagine myself slipping inside, going deeper into the darkness and the silence.

The thought doesn't comfort me, though. In fact, the longer I stare at the caves the more I imagine something with flat, cold, unblinking eyes staring back at me from the shadows.

They get angry if you look at them, Scott said.

Also: *they bite.*

I shudder and turn away. As I do so, at the edge of my vision, I see a squat black shape with red eyes watching me from the roadway below.

My head snaps round so quickly that something twists in my neck with a gristly sound, releasing a hot burst of pain that fills my vision with tumbling black ash. I blink frantically to clear it, but it takes several seconds before I'm able to see that the black shape is no longer there — or perhaps it never was.

Even so, I scan the area thoroughly before I'm convinced I'm alone, and then make my way not down the sloping garden, but across it, heading for the hammock slung between two of a cluster of fruit trees to my right. Once there, I'm hidden from the road by an overlapping screen of trees and bushes, and also from the caves, not only by more trees but also by the protruding edge of the house directly behind and above me.

The hammock is a scoop of mesh-like material, which I have to clear of leaves before I'm able to clamber in. It sways alarmingly at first, but as soon as I get myself settled it moulds itself around my body and is one of the most comfortable things I've ever laid in. I open my book, which is one of a series I'm reading about three boys who solve bizarre and baffling mysteries. In this one the boys buy an old magician's trunk in an auction and discover a skull inside, which seems to talk to them in the dark, giving them clues to the whereabouts of a horde of stolen money. At first I'm too unsettled to concentrate on the story, but after a while my surroundings fade away and I become engrossed.

I don't realize someone has crept up behind me until a shadow falls over me. I jump, then try to twist round and sit up, which makes the trees supporting the hammock creak as the hammock sways from side to side, almost tipping me out. Though I don't know what they look like I expect to see one of the night people

(*they bite*)

standing there, but it's only Angie. She's scowling, though I know straight away she's not angry with me.

"What's up?" I ask.

"Dad is such a pig."

I immediately feel that hollow, sick feeling in my stomach again. "Why? What's happened?"

"He hit Mum."

The world seems to tilt at the sheer wrongness of what Angie has said, and for a moment I feel so dizzy I can't think straight. "What?" I say. "When? Just now?"

She frowns, and this time it *is* me she's angry at. "Of course not, you idiot." She gestures towards the empty space on the road in front of the cottage where the car is usually parked. "Dad's not here now, is he?"

"No," I concede, feeling foolish. "When then?"

"Last night. He punched her in the arm and the ribs. She's got bruises here and here." She points to her upper forearm and the left side of her chest.

I'm appalled. Boys aren't supposed to hit girls. And men are *definitely* not supposed to hit women. "He can't do that!" is all I can think of to say.

Angie's face is grim. "He already has. He's a fucking pig."

She spits out the words. I want to be as angry as she is, but all I feel is dismay and confusion. "But why?" I say. "What did he do it for?"

"Because Mum wouldn't give him what he wanted. She didn't want to. She didn't *have* to either."

She says this fiercely, as if I've contradicted her. I'm still confused. My thoughts feel as if they're bouncing all over the place. "What do you mean? What *did* he want?"

She looks at me almost pityingly. "Grow up, Frank. What do you think?"

When I just stare at her she virtually spits the word in my face: "Sex."

Dismay turns to distress. I want to curl up, shrivel away from what she's telling me. I don't want to think about this, don't want to think about Mum and Dad *doing it*. I know it's childish, but I just want to put my fingers in my ears and close my eyes and go la-la-la so that I can't hear or see anything.

But I don't. I don't want Angie to think even less of me. I feel as though enough of a gulf has formed between us in the last few days as it is. And so I say, "Oh. Right."

Still she huffs, as though I've said the wrong thing, failed some sort of test. Then abruptly she turns away, craning her neck to look back at the house. "I'm going in the caves. You coming?"

My dismay increases. *As if things aren't bad enough*, I think. "What, now?"

"Yes, now."

I grope for an excuse not to go that won't annoy her. "What about Mum?"

"She's sleeping. She's taken some pills."

I didn't know Mum took pills to sleep, or maybe she just means painkillers. "Well, what about what Gary and Scott told us yesterday? About the Fay?"

"What about it?"

Her face is like stone, her mouth set in a stubborn line.

"Well... they said the Fay were dangerous. They said they bite and steal children."

She gives a tiny shake of the head, as if she's disappointed. "Are you scared of everything, Frank?"

"No," I say defensively.

"So are you coming or not?"

It's clear that she can't be dissuaded. Although I feel ashamed I shake my head. "I like it out here in the sunshine. I'm comfortable. I want to read my book."

If she smiled and said 'Okay' or 'I'll see you later' it would be all right, but she doesn't. She stares at me a moment longer and then she turns and walks away.

I consider calling after her. I consider *going* after her. I almost do. I feel guilty and ashamed and cowardly, but then all at once a wave of resentment washes over me. Why *should* I do what Angie wants? Why *should* she get her own way? What right has she got to judge me just because I don't want to poke about in a stupid dark cave with her?

So I slump back into the hammock, wriggling my body to get comfortable, and I open my book again. I feel the sun on my face and I listen to the lazy drone of bees and I tell myself *this* is what summer is all about; *this* is what we came here for.

I start to read, and after a while I feel my eyelids getting heavy. I don't realize I've fallen asleep until someone speaks my name.

I open my eyes and notice immediately that the light has changed. The sun is lower in the sky and the shadows are more stretched-out. A light breeze has picked up, which, although it's not exactly cold, still makes me shiver.

A dark figure is standing over me, silhouetted against the sky. I half-sit up and shadows slide away from its face and I realize it's Mum.

"Hi," I say.

She smiles. "Hi yourself." She looks around. "All alone?"

I nod, stretch. Despite the heat I notice she's wearing a long-sleeved top. "I must have fallen asleep."

"I can see that."

"What time is it?"

"Almost six. I came to tell you that dinner's nearly ready. You need to come in and wash your hands."

"Okay," I say and ease myself out of the hammock, causing the trees to creak again. "Is Angie back?"

Mum frowns. "Back from where?"

I feel a prickle of unease. How long is it since I last saw Angie? Three hours? Four? "She went into the caves ages ago. Hasn't she come out?"

"Not to my knowledge," Mum says, and purses her lips. "Why didn't you go with her?"

"I didn't want to," I say, my voice rising defensively. "I wanted to read my book."

"I don't like her going into those caves alone," Mum says. "Didn't you try to stop her?"

I shrug. "How could I have? She wouldn't have listened to me."

She snorts a half-laugh, though she's clearly worried. "That's true. Got a mind of her own, that one."

I almost ask Mum whose mind she'd expect Angie to have, but now isn't the time. I glance towards the road, but I can't see whether the car's there because of the screen of trees. "Is Dad back?" I ask, realizing that if Mum says no I'll be happier than if she says yes.

She grimaces slightly, but nods. "Yes, he's back."

"Is everything all right?" I ask.

She looks at me so fiercely that I suspect she ordered Angie not to tell me anything. "What do you mean?"

"I mean… after what happened before. At lunch."

She relaxes a little. "Well, peace has been restored for now. He brought me flowers."

She says this a little bitterly, as though it's no compensation for what he's done. Then she frowns and looks towards the caves, though they can't be seen from where we are. "Never mind about your dad. It's Angie I'm worried about."

"I'm sure she'll turn up," I say. "She probably just wanted to be on her own for a bit. Have you checked her room? Maybe she's already inside."

She's not inside, though, and so me, Mum and Dad head over to the caves to look for her. Dad's angry, though I don't know whether that's because he's worried or because he finds Angie's disappearance an inconvenience. He stomps from cave entrance to cave entrance, yelling her name and shining his torch into the darkness.

"That bloody girl," he growls. "I'll give her a bloody good hiding when she turns up."

"No, you won't," Mum says tersely. Then her body and her face seem to sag as she peers into the nearest cave entrance. "Oh, God, where is she, George? What if she's hurt? What if she's..." Instead of putting it into words she shakes her head and wafts a hand in front of her face.

"She'll be fine," Dad says as if he's too obstinate to accept anything else.

"She's probably just gone too far into the caves to hear us, Mum," I say.

Mum looks at me, stricken, her eyes red though she hasn't cried yet. "She could be lost, you mean?"

Dad flashes me a scathing look, as if I've made things worse. "Of course she's not lost. She won't have just wandered off. She's not daft."

"Where is she then?" Mum snaps. "Tell me that."

But Dad can't, and so despite him telling her that it's too soon she goes inside to call the police, leaving me and Dad alone. He looks at me like all this is my fault, but instead of telling me off he mutters, "Bloody women. They're more trouble than they're worth." It's as if he's sharing a confidence with me, as if the simple fact that we're both male means that for once we're united against a common enemy. I don't agree with what he's said — in fact, it makes me so angry that I want to scream at him. I want to tell him that I wish *he* was the one who was lost. But I force myself to smile even though I know I'm betraying Mum and Angie by doing so.

Because it's better than just standing around, Dad leads the way further into the caves. Even though I'm nervous after what Scott told us yesterday, a part of me *wants* the Fay to appear, maybe in the form of a pack of black dogs with red eyes, and attack Dad. I nurse a fantasy of them leaping on him and tearing him apart, his screams echoing off the walls as I turn and flee. Immediately I'm ashamed of the thought. If the Fay *were* here, and if they *did* attack Dad, then wasn't it likely they'd have attacked Angie too?

Some of the caves are deep, and after a while they branch off in different directions. Me and Dad look in three, shouting Angie's name as we go, but then he says, "This is bloody hopeless."

When we come out, Mum's waiting for us. She's called the police and she tells us they'll be sending someone soon. Dad suggests going back to the house and eating dinner while we wait, but Mum looks at him with disgust.

"How can you even *think* of eating at a time like this?" she says.

Anger flashes across his face, but then he seems to remember that he's trying to make up for his earlier behaviour and so he moulds his features into a sympathetic expression. "We've got to eat, love," he says, "got to keep our strength up. No point starving ourselves."

"I couldn't eat a thing," Mum says coldly.

"Maybe not, but the lad needs something." He nods at me as if to confirm who he's talking about.

In the same cold voice, Mum says, "There's shepherd's pie in the oven if you want it. I'm going to wait here for the police."

"We won't be long," Dad says. "We'll just have a quick bite. Won't we, Frank?"

I don't know what to do. I *am* a bit hungry, but I don't want Mum to think I don't care about Angie. And I don't want her to think I'm taking sides with Dad against her either.

Mum's not stupid, though. She can tell the dilemma I'm in just by looking at my face. She smiles and touches my shoulder. "Your dad's right. You need something to eat. Off you go."

The shepherd's pie's not that warm, and it's gone a bit dry round the edges, but Dad serves it up anyway. He looks at the peas and carrots, which are sitting in cooling water on a pan on the stove, and pulls a face.

"Do you want beans?" he asks.

I shake my head and Dad pulls another face, as if that means he can't have any either. As I put HP sauce on my pie, he bangs his plate down so hard on the table that I think it's going to break, but it doesn't, and then we eat together in silence. I shovel my food in as quickly as I can because Dad makes me nervous and I don't want to be alone with him for any longer than I have to. As soon as I've swallowed the last mouthful I mutter, "May I get down from the table, please," which is what Mum always insists we ask, but before he can answer we both hear the sound of an approaching car.

He glances at me, then jumps up and is out of the house before I can move. By the time I wriggle out of my seat and hurry after him, two policemen are climbing the steps towards the house. They don't seem to be hurrying, and for a second I can't help wondering whether that's because they're scared of the caves, or even because they know that Angie will never be found. The policeman in front has got grey hair and a grey moustache, and is older and fatter than his partner, who has brown curly hair and such a smooth face that he doesn't look as if he needs to shave.

I'm surprised when Dad grins and almost bounds forward as if he's eager to please the policemen. "Thanks for coming," he says.

Mum looks less welcoming. She asks, "Are there only two of you?"

"For now, madam," says the older policeman. "I understand your daughter's gone AWOL?"

"She's gone *missing*," Mum says and I wonder whether it's only because she's so worried about Angie that she seems cross. "No one's seen her for hours."

Instead of searching the caves the policemen ask lots of questions. And no matter how agitated Mum gets, which is very, they stay calm, especially the older one.

"Are you quite sure she went in the caves?" the older policeman asks.

Dad stabs a finger at me. "The lad says she did."

When everyone looks at me I blush and my mind goes momentarily blank. I nod and that seems to loosen my thoughts, and I say, "She asked me if I wanted to go in the caves, but I didn't, so she went by herself."

"And what time was this?" the policeman asks, and I tell him. "And did you actually see her enter the caves?"

When I tell him I didn't he suggests that she could be anywhere.

She could be in the woods. She could be staying away to punish Mum and Dad for arguing.

"Our Angie isn't like that," Mum says fiercely. "She's a thoughtful girl. Compassionate. She's not spiteful."

The older policeman smiles, deep wrinkles appearing round his eyes and mouth. "I'm sure she isn't, Mrs Ryan," he says, "but kids that age... they get confused. Sometimes they need time on their own."

He looks as me as if hoping I'll confirm what he says, but I just stare at him.

"Be that as it may," Mum says, "the fact is, she's missing and soon it'll get dark. So what are you going to do about it?"

"Pat," Dad says gently, as if he's the calm one in the relationship.

"I'm sure she'll turn up, Mrs Ryan," the younger policeman says, "once she's hungry enough."

"And what if she doesn't?" Mum snaps. "What if she's lost? What if she's lying hurt somewhere? What if someone's taken her?" Her face twitches, almost crumbles, as she gives voice to her deepest fears, and then she takes a deep breath and continues, "What's the point of waiting to see if she comes back? Because if she doesn't it'll then be too dark to look for her."

The older policeman raises his hands and I notice with a shock that the little finger on his left hand is missing. I wonder how he lost it? In the war? In a fight with a burglar?

"I understand your concern, Mrs Ryan," he says.

"Understand it?" Mum says, and now her voice is shrill; she's almost shrieking. "How can you understand it? It's my daughter that's missing, not yours."

In the end some more policemen come, and they've got dogs and big torches and they search the caves and the woods.

But by the time it gets dark Angie's still missing.

I stay up as long as I'm allowed, but even when I finally go to bed she's still not back.

*

I'm in the cave, walking. My footsteps clop on the stone floor like horses' hooves, but I can't seem to quieten them, no matter how softly I tread. Even though it's dark and I have no torch, I can see perfectly well. There is a yellow-brown shimmer to the walls, as if the cave is generating its own light-source.

I'm scared. The muscles of my body feel stiff with tension. It makes it hard to move fluently. I know that if I'm called upon to run I probably won't be able to. I don't know why I'm moving ever deeper into the cave, but I can't seem to help myself. Something is compelling me, drawing me in. I can hear sounds around me. Harsh scrapings and rattlings and something that sounds like the caw of a bird. They echo, distorted. It's hard to tell how close or far away they are. Perhaps they're all around me, perhaps I'm surrounded. I squint into the shimmering gloom, but I can't seem to focus properly. There are too many sharp angles, too many uneven surfaces. They slither with light and shadow.

Then I'm somewhere else. There's no real sense of progression, but all at once I'm in a vast cavern. It may be the cavern I saw before, when I was with Angie, but I'm not sure. If it is, I'm viewing it from a different angle — from the bottom of the valley, my feet planted next to a sluggish trickle of water. I crane my neck to peer at the black scars in the rock face that sweeps up ahead of me. I see movement.

Rocks trickling. Tiny landslides, that's all. But I know that I'm being watched. I suddenly take fright, and turn, and try to scramble up the slope behind me. But it's like glass, smooth and slippery and impossible to climb. My heart pounds in my ears. It's so loud that it makes the rock walls shiver. Perhaps they'll shatter, I think. Perhaps a tunnel will open in front of me and I'll be able to escape. I try to shout for help, but my throat is tight, clogged, and I can't make a sound above a pitiful croak. For some reason I look to my right, along the length of the black stream that cuts through the centre of the cavern. There's something there in the gloom. Something that paws at the walls, as if blind, as it makes its way towards me.

It's maggot-white and its skin glistens, gleams. It's thin and shaped like a man, but it seems boneless, sliding along the rock wall as if moulding itself like a jellyfish to the rough bulges and jags and crevices. It has no face that I can see, but behind the featureless, gelid mask something shifts and swirls. It reminds me of the constantly changing colours in an oil slick and it seems to possess a queasy and dreadful significance.

They bite, I think, and then someone calls out my name: "Frank! Frank!"

It distracts me enough for the thing in the cave to stretch out an impossibly long white hand and paw at my arm.

I scream and my eyes tear open.

I'm in bed, but I'm not out of the dream. Something is looming over me, but it jerks back when I wake with a shout. Then I hear Mum's voice, rushed and breathless. "It's all right, Frank, don't panic. It's only me."

A lamp clicks on and I shield my eyes from the glare. I don't know what time it is or why I'm being woken up or what's going on, but when I ungum my lips all I can manage is, "Wha?"

"It's the middle of the night," Mum says, and I can hear the eagerness in her voice, the happiness, "but I thought you'd like to know."

The glare starts to fade and through it I see her wide, gleaming eyes, her flushed cheeks.

"It's Angie," she says. "She's back. She's come back to us!"

*

I drive down to the bottom of the cul-de-sac, but there's nowhere to park. It's a tight manouvre to turn the car round again, involving lots of edging forwards and backwards, and by the time I eventually manage it I'm sweating from the effort and the stress. I head back the way I've come, crawling along at less than 5mph as I scan both sides of the road for a parking space. Because this is a new estate there are lots of young families living here, and I hope no one thinks I'm a paedophile on the hunt for potential victims.

Eventually I find a space, though it's at least four hundred metres from the house. I pull in, detach the CD player and lock it in the glove compartment, then hook the two ends of the crook-lock around the gear stick and clutch. The present, which is wrapped in pink paper with white rabbits on it, is sitting on the passenger seat, and the bottle of Chardonnay, which I hope hasn't lost much of its chill on the twenty-minute journey over, is wedged into the central well between a couple of wadded-up tea towels.

Picking up these items I open the car door and unfold myself into the sunlight.

Even though it's a boiling hot day I'm wearing a shirt — albeit a short-sleeved one — and jeans. I would have worn shorts and a T-shirt, but I never thought to ask Angie what the other parents would be wearing, so I decided to play it safe. As I stretch I feel the sweaty fabric unpeel itself from my back and hope the stain doesn't look too unsightly. At least the walk round to the house will dry it out a little, unless the exercise makes me sweat even more.

As I lock the car door and start walking I hope, not for the first time, that the wrapping paper around Aspen's present won't be considered inappropriate. I tell myself that just because it's got rabbits on it doesn't necessarily mean that people will think I've used paper left over from Easter. I haven't, of course, though I didn't even make the connection until it was too late. I'm not sure you can even *get* Easter paper, but all the same I do now wish I'd bought paper with 'Happy Birthday' written on it.

Not that Aspen will mind, of course. She's only one. She won't really mind about the present either, though I'm slightly anxious about what the other parents will think. I'm not used to buying presents for small children and I don't really know what is and isn't considered acceptable. I've bought Aspen something that seemed to me both fun and educational, a sort of interactive plastic zoo shaped like a small but chunky computer screen. The zoo is full of friendly-looking cartoon animals and it makes funny noises and has buttons you can push and things you can spin round.

Angie and Chris live in a three-bedroomed house that is tucked away in the left-hand corner at the end of the cul-de-sac. It's a nice place, but to me it always looks as though it's trying to hide, or at least not to be noticed. Perhaps it only looks that way because I've transferred Angie's personality and characteristics to where she lives. I find it ironic that for the first ten years of her life she was the confident one, the reckless one, the go-getter, and now she's withdrawn and secretive.

On the right hand side of the house there's a gate between the edge of the building and the fence that borders the property. Beyond the gate I can hear laughter and chatter. I steel myself. I don't know any of these people and I know from what Chris has told me that the majority of them will be young couples with small children. There may be one or two grandparents there as well, though I doubt there'll be any other 'singletons' (as Chris's friend Karen calls them) like me. Although I will feel like an outsider, I know that this will also be a relief. I was once persuaded to take Karen out on a date and found it an intensely uncomfortable experience. It was nothing to do with Karen, it was just the falseness of the situation. The expectations of other people, the obligation to get on, was, to me, too much of a burden. It was like trying to enjoy yourself with a rucksack full of rocks on your back.

With the present under my right arm and the bottle of wine in my left hand I fumble the gate open and step through. A flag-stoned path edged with gravel leads up the side of the house towards a wedge of sunlight which angles in from the back garden. I know this is my last chance to turn back and for a moment I actually consider it. Then I think of Angie, of how little we see each other these days, which I tell myself is because of work commitments for me and family commitments for her, and I stroll along the path with a brashness I don't feel, forcing my face into a smile as I step into the sunlight.

For an instant it's as crushingly intimidating as I expect it to be — a mass of unfamiliar faces breaking off from laughter-filled conversations to peer at me with curiosity and suspicion — and then I hear my name being called and I turn my head and see Chris on the other side of the sun-drenched lawn, waving a pair of metal tongs at me. He's standing behind a thin curtain of smoke — a barbecue, from which drifts a mouth-watering smell of roasting meat. The barbecue is ringed with brightly-coloured plastic cones, denoting a no-go area for those children — presumably the elder brothers and sisters of the one year olds like Aspen — who are racing around in shrieking, sweaty, excitable groups.

I raise the bottle by way of greeting, then wonder whether, because I'm single and childless, this might be construed by some of the parents as an indication that I've come here to get drunk. Sheepishly I make my way over to Chris, avoiding eye contact with the strangers I'm weaving through.

The garden, which is mostly lawn, is surrounded by a high hedge. From one corner comes an almost comical creak of springs as several children bounce on a trampoline shrouded in what looks like a gigantic mosquito net. Most of the babies, including Aspen, have been deposited in a huge blow-up playpen in the centre of the lawn, where they sit or crawl like a litter of puppies, distracted by simple, primary-coloured plastic toys or adults who lean forward to coo at them. Most of the snatches of conversation I hear are about children, though one quartet of hearty men, who all wear knee-length shorts and sandals and sip from bottles of light-coloured beer, are talking about rugby and laughing a great deal.

By the time I reach Chris I'm sweating.

"Hey, mate, thanks for coming," he says, turning over burgers with the tongs.

"Thanks for inviting me," I say. "It seems to be going well."

Chris nods. He's changed a bit since I first met him over ten years ago. He's a little fatter now around the stomach and neck and his once-shaggy hair is neatly trimmed. He's lost the facial hair too, and although he still wears glasses they are no longer the light-sensitive ones that I couldn't help thinking always made him look a bit seedy. Today he's wearing Police sunglasses, which mask his eyes entirely, over a Fruit of the Loom T-shirt and jeans cut off at the knees. He's grinning like he's overjoyed to see me, which I find unnerving.

"It is," he says. "So, how are you doing?"

"Fine," I say, not sure how much detail he wants. "I didn't know you knew so many people."

He flips a couple of sausages and then leans towards me. "Shall I let you in on a little secret?"

I shrug, and not altogether enthusiastically say, "Go on then."

"I hardly know anyone here. A few of these people are neighbours, who I occasionally say hi to, but most are women from Aspen's mother and toddler group, which I've never been to, and their husbands."

"Right," I say, unsure what else to add. Should I be relieved that Chris and I are allies in our ignorance or alarmed that if I want to get to know any of these people I'll have to do so off my own bat?

Eventually I say, "Oh well. Looks as though everyone's getting on okay. And the kids are enjoying themselves."

Chris nods and half-laughs and then indicates the bottle I'm holding. "Did you bring that for Aspen?"

Just in time I realize he's joking and I grin. "Thought you and Angie might be in need of this by tonight."

He grins back. "I'd say that's a distinct possibility."

"Where is she, by the way?"

I'm not sure because I can't see his eyes, but a troubled look seems to pass briefly across his face. "She's inside. Making a salad and getting plates and things organized."

"I'll go and say hi and give her a hand," I say.

"Okay." Chris hesitates, and then as I move away, he says, "Frank?"

I turn back.

"A bit later on... can we have a little chat?"

I look at him a moment, but his eyeless face gives nothing away. I shrug, as though by being casual it will make the request less ominous. "Sure," I say.

As Chris said, I find Angie in the kitchen. She's alone. She's sitting at the big wooden table, staring into space, a kitchen knife in her hand. In front of her is a chopping board, on which are pak choi, tomatoes, radishes and red and yellow peppers, all neatly sliced. Beyond that is a big, empty salad bowl and a still-sealed transparent bag of croutons and the ingredients for making a dressing — olive oil, balsamic vinegar, honey, black pepper...

"Hi," I say, and Angie jumps, the knife jerking up in her hand, the blade flashing in the sunlight.

She stares at me without recognition for perhaps a second and then her thin, sallow face relaxes into a smile. "Oh, Frank, hi. Lovely to see you. Thanks so much for coming."

"Wouldn't have missed it for the world," I say, wishing our opening exchange hadn't been so trite. I cross to the fridge, open it, and slide the bottle of wine inside, then put Aspen's present on the counter between a toaster and a coffee percolator. I cross to my sister, who by now has placed the knife down on the chopping board and has half-swivelled round on her stool. She raises her arms towards me like a small child who wants to be picked up.

I hug her and she clutches me fiercely, turning her face aside and crushing the side of her head against my chest. I can smell her hair. Although it looks stringy it smells of peach, or perhaps melon, shampoo.

"How are you doing?" I ask.

Her voice is muffled. "Not so good."

I kiss the top of her head. "Why not? It all seems to be going great out there. It's a beautiful day. Everyone seems happy."

She sighs and I fall silent, giving her the room to answer in her own time. From outside comes a guffawing wave of laughter from the rugby aficionados. How long before one of Angie's 'friends' comes in to check on her? If Angie doesn't tell me what's wrong before then she probably never will.

Finally she says, "I can't help thinking..."

"What?" I prompt gently.

She sighs again, deeper this time, and pulls away from me. I wonder if I've already pushed too hard, but she doesn't look reluctant to speak, just thoughtful. She busies herself transferring the salad ingredients from the chopping board to the bowl, cupping her hands as though scooping water from a sink. Her hands are delicate, bird-like, almost translucently pale, but dark pink, raw-looking, at the fingertips. I watch her silently, waiting for her to speak. At last she does.

"I sometimes ask myself," she says, with a note of weariness in her voice, as though she has been over this issue many times, "whether I deserve all this. And usually the answer is no, I don't deserve any of it."

She falls silent and I stare at her. I'm not sure exactly what she's saying. Is she resentful of the twenty-odd years of emotional instability she's had to put up with, or is she claiming she's unworthy of the bounty that has come her way — her husband and daughter, her lovely home, her settled life? I wish I knew without having to ask. I wish our minds were instantly in tune like they used to be — or as I *recall* they used to be.

Having to ask feels like a failing, but tentatively I say, "What do you mean?"

She wafts a hand to indicate her surroundings. She has tomato seeds stuck to her fingers.

"All this," she says with a frown of impatience. "It's all too good for me. I don't deserve it. Chris is too good for me. Aspen's too good for me. It's not right that I should have all this."

"Don't be daft," I say. "What makes you think that?"

"Nothing *makes* me think it," she says. "I just do. I just... I know it's true, that's all."

I shake my head. "You're being too hard on yourself. Of *course* you deserve this. You've worked hard for it. Chris loves you."

She turns away with a sound that is somewhere between a snort and a sob and crosses to the sink and turns on the tap. As she rolls up her sleeves in order to wash her hands I see the scattering of old scars on her arms, white and puckered.

Like the marks made by small, sharp teeth.

Later I speak to Chris.

It's around 4pm. Everyone's eaten and the big black plastic dustbin by the patio doors is full of crumpled waxy paper plates smeared with ketchup and mayonnaise, disposable drinks cups and plastic cutlery. A blue recycling container next to the bin brims with empty beer and wine bottles. Around an hour ago Angie emerged from the kitchen carrying a big pink cake with a single candle in the centre, which she ended up blowing out herself once everyone had finished singing 'Happy Birthday' to a bemused Aspen. The cake was cut up and handed out mostly to the children, the majority of whom, tired and grumpy after too much food and excitement, have now been taken home by their parents. Those that are left are either asleep or draped over the furniture in the front room like a pride of lion cubs, quietly watching TV. They watch DVDs of the cartoons I remember from my childhood — *Scooby Doo* and *Wacky Races* and *The Road Runner.*

The four rugby fans, drunk now and swaying slightly, are still here, though their wives have now drifted across to join them. After handing out the cake, Angie used an increasingly fractious Aspen as an excuse to retreat back indoors, promising she would be back once she had fed and changed her daughter and put her down for her afternoon nap. I wonder if I am the only one who thought Angie's smile was unconvincing as she said this. Certainly she has not yet re-emerged and it is now reaching the stage where her absence is being noticed. Chris has already had to promise to pass the thanks and farewells of several departing couples on to his wife, and he has had to discourage another mother from checking on Angie by telling her that sometimes it takes Aspen a while to settle and her presence would only disrupt the procedure.

He and I sit side by side on fold-out garden chairs, close enough to the cooling barbecue for Chris to gently warn away any children who might venture into the danger area. Because the shadow of the tall hedge to our left stretches across us, Chris has pushed his sunglasses up onto his forehead, revealing eyes whose whites look pink and wet. He has been drinking red wine steadily over the course of the afternoon and it has stained his lips and teeth a dirty maroon. He is not really drunk, but he *has* become a little maudlin, to the extent that I'm not sure whether his pink eyes are due to barbecue smoke, alcohol or contained emotion. He speaks quietly but passionately about Angie, slurring only the occasional word as he stares down into his glass. He has spent almost their entire relationship being worried about her, which is one of the many things I like about him — his unswerving love for and unconditional dedication to my sister. He tells me that Angie has been suffering from post natal depression, which he describes as 'pretty bloody chronic'. He says that entire days have passed during which she has been unable to stop crying; that she has questioned the point of her existence on many occasions, and has even berated Chris for his loyalty when he would be far better off without her.

"Has she actually threatened to take her own life?" I ask.

Chris thinks about this for a long time, staring down into his glass as if the answer might be found there.

At length he shifts in his seat, the chair creaking as he pushes his slumped body a little more upright.

"Not in so many words," he says, "but she's inferred it. It grinds me down, Frank. It's fucking scary."

"I'm sure," I say. "And how is she with Aspen?"

"Oh, she's great." (in his North Eastern accent he pronounces it 'grey-ut') "In fact, if anything, she's *too* protective. She thinks the world's a big, evil place that's out to get her baby."

She's probably right, I think, but I don't say it. Instead I nod and sip my cranberry juice.

Hesitantly Chris says, "She blames hersel', y'know, for what happened between your mam and dad. Them splitting up and then... afterwards."

A burst of laughter erupts from the rugby fans and their wives, and for a moment I feel a fierce, seething hatred for them.

"She has no reason to," I say. "If Dad hated anyone it was me." I clench my teeth against the admission and force it into a smile. "But the truth is, it wasn't anyone's fault. Nothing that either me or Angie or Mum could have done would have changed what Dad did."

Chris is nodding, but he looks miserable. He raises his glass to his mouth so abruptly that wine splashes on to his hand.

"Aye, well, I wish you could make *her* believe that," he says.

*

"Frank." The voice is urgent and is accompanied by someone shaking me awake. "Frank, love, come on."

I sit up in bed, blinking, my mouth dry. I'm twelve years old and fear is the first emotion that grips me. What I'm scared of is Dad, or more particularly the violence that spills out of him so readily and viciously these days. The fact that I haven't yet been on the receiving end of it makes no difference. Mum might bear the punches and kicks, but Angie and I have been scarred by the mental blows. There are no worse sounds in the world than the crunch and smack of flesh on flesh; Mum's screams of pain and pleas for mercy; the crashes and thuds as her body is sent reeling against the furniture and walls. And there are no worse sights than her bruised ribs and her split and swollen face, and by her obvious pain as she shuffles and limps about, trying to make light of what has happened. And there is nothing more shaming than being frozen by your own fear, your own inability to act. I can't help but feel that by standing by and doing nothing I am somehow compliant in Dad's violence, even though I find it sickening.

My bedroom is in darkness, but my door is ajar and light spills in from the landing. Framed by the light is Angie's thin figure, her shoulders hunched and her arms crossed as though she is cold. There is something by her feet. I blink again and see that it's a suitcase.

"What's happening?" I ask.

Mum rises from the bed, placing a hand in the small of her back, wincing against the pain. Her voice is muffled because of her swollen lip. "Get dressed, Frank. Quickly now. We're leaving."

Confusion causes my voice to sharpen. "Leaving? Where are we going?"

"Somewhere your dad can't get at us." She looks at me, and her face is all at once so serious, so honest, so lacking in guile that it frightens me. "I can't take any more of it, Frank."

It is the first time, as far as I can remember, that she has truly spoken to me as an adult. I have dreamed of us running away from Dad, of somehow ejecting him from our lives, but now that the fantasy is becoming a reality I feel alarmed, even resentful.

"What about my things?" I say, looking around my room. "My clothes and toys and books?"

"I've packed a case for you," Mum says. "It's got all the clothes you'll need in it. You've got ten minutes to get dressed and choose a few more bits and bobs. But not too much, Frank. Whatever you bring you'll have to carry."

Part of me is appalled that I'm anything but supportive of Mum, but I hear myself saying, "What about school?"

Patiently Mum says, "You'll have to have a bit of time off, but hopefully, once we're settled, things will get back to normal."

I still haven't swung my legs out of bed. "Why do we have to do this now?"

Mum looks anguished, and instantly I feel ashamed. I'm about to apologise when from the doorway, in a low and bitter voice, Angie mutters, "Stay here with Dad then if you don't want to come. But me and Mum are going whether you like it or not."

I feel stung by her contempt, but I try to dispel it by throwing back the covers, defying the chill of the November air. "Of course I want to come," I say.

"Ten minutes," Mum says and leaves me to it. I bustle around the room, getting dressed, throwing a few things — mainly books — into the vinyl shoulder bag I take to school, which bears the legend 'XXI Olympiad Montreal 1976'.

When I look at my clock, which I also stuff into my bag, I'm surprised to find it's only 10:30pm. For some reason I thought it was the early hours of the morning. Then I realize Dad must be at the pub, which means he'll be home in half an hour or so. I imagine him finishing off his last pint, the alcohol turning to blackness and rage inside him. For the last minute or so I fly around the room in a panic, feeling as though we're making ready to flee in the face of an oncoming storm. Dad is a hurricane, a whirlwind, with the ability to tear buildings apart. When I hear a roar outside I think for a moment it's him, that he's found out what we're doing, that we're too late. But then the roar settles into the growling chug of an idling engine and Mum shouts my name up the stairs.

"Coming!" I shout and heave my now-heavy bag up on to my shoulder and cross the room to the door. At the threshold I look back — at my unmade bed, my now slightly depleted shelves of books, my record player with its peeling grey lid, my posters (*The Goodies, Starsky and Hutch, Jaws*), my stack of board games under the window. When will I see it all again? When will I next see Dad, if ever? Where will I sleep tonight? I feel as though the foundations of my life are crumbling, as though I'm about to fall.

"Goodbye," I whisper and pull the door closed behind me. Then I run down the stairs, towards Mum and Angie and the waiting taxi.

*

Angie's in the hospital. Mum says there's nothing to worry about, they're just checking her over. When she got back last night her hands and face and clothes were dirty and the pocket of her jeans was torn. Her arm was bleeding too from what Mum says looked like an animal bite. When Mum asked her about it, Angie said she couldn't remember how it happened. All she says she does remember is getting lost in the caves and falling asleep. She doesn't remember waking up or how she found her way back. It wasn't the police who found her; she just appeared, walking out of the caves like a sleepwalker. Mum says her eyes were wide but blank and scary-looking. She didn't smile and she didn't cry and she moved slowly and stiffly like a robot.

The police talked to her, but they couldn't get much out of her. In the end they told Mum and Dad to get her cleaned up and to take her to the hospital for a check-up, and then they left. That was when I went back to bed, and this morning when I woke up Angie was gone. Mum told me she'd given Angie a bath and Angie had sat there like a doll, staring into space, while Mum washed her. Mum said it was creepy. She wondered if Angie had been attacked, but she said there was no sign of it apart from that bite on Angie's arm, which she said looked like a bite from a cat or maybe a fox. She made Dad drive Angie to the hospital, and when they got there the doctor who examined her decided to keep her in overnight 'for observation'. They cleaned up the bite and gave her a tetanus injection and the doctor told Dad that he was worried about Angie's 'lack of emotional response' and that if she didn't show any improvement he would recommend that she undergo 'psychiatric evaluation'.

"I bloody told him," Dad said when he related the story to me and Mum at breakfast the next morning, "I told him, our Angie's no nutter."

"And what did *he* say?" Mum asked calmly.

Dad waved his hand as though dismissing her question, or perhaps the doctor's reply. "He said something about trauma. About internalizing something-or-other. I can't remember. It was a load of bollocks. You know what these people are like."

When I see Angie later that morning my first thought is that she looks like a ghost. She's sitting up in bed, staring into space, not doing anything. She wears a white hospital gown and her right arm is bandaged from her wrist all the way up to her elbow. Even her skin looks white, which makes her eyes look as black as oil.

When me and Mum pull up chairs and sit by her bed and say hello she turns her head very slowly. Her lips, which look as though they've had all the redness squeezed out of them, take so long to curve into a smile it's as though she's using the muscles for the first time. As Mum chats away, asking Angie how she's feeling and whether she's slept all right and what she's had to eat, I stare at my sister, fascinated by how waxy her skin looks and how dark and flat and brittle her hair seems. I imagine reaching out and pushing my fingers into her cheek, the flesh yielding like soft putty; I imagine taking her hair in my fingers and snapping off the ends like thin twigs.

Angie answers Mum's questions in a soft voice, using as few words as possible. When I show her the comics I've brought for her — *The Dandy* and *Whizzer and Chips* and *TV Comic* — she says thanks but seems uninterested, even though she normally likes them as much as I do.

Mum asks about a hundred questions before she gets round to the one she *really* wants to ask. "Have you remembered what happened?"

Angie shakes her head. Then she says, "I'm thirsty. Can you ask the nurse to bring some water?"

Mum looks exasperated, and I think for a minute that she'll only agree to Angie's request if Angie opens up to her. Then she nods abruptly and says, "Of course," and goes off to find a nurse.

As soon as she's gone my heart starts thumping hard in my chest and I lean forward, and before I can chicken out I say, "Are you really you?"

For the first time Angie shows a flicker of surprise. "What do you mean?"

The next question is even harder to ask, but I force it out. "Are you a changeling?"

She stares at me for what seems like ages, and I hold my breath, then quietly she says, "He was right, you know."

"Who?" I ask, confused.

"Scott."

I look up the length of the ward. Mum is talking to a nurse, pointing towards Angie's bed. She'll be back any second.

"What about?" I ask.

I sense Mum walking back towards us, and I think that Angie's not going to answer in time.

But then she says in a murmur, "They don't like people staring at them."

*

It's Christmas Eve 2004. For once I'm here with Angie and her family. Mum's here too, but she's gone to bed, as has Chris and of course the girls.

Six-year-old Aspen is so excited about tomorrow that it took her hours to get to sleep. A fear that Santa Claus wouldn't leave any presents if she was still awake when he arrived led to tears before exhaustion finally claimed her. Three-year-old India is excited too, though I suspect she doesn't quite know why. She's excited because her sister is excited, and because the house is full of glittery ornaments and twinkling lights, most of which adorn the tree in the corner, which exudes the seasonal waft of pine.

Even now, with my fortieth birthday less than six months away, I find that smell deeply evocative. To me it is redolent of innocence, of simplicity, of happiness, of the deep and delicious thrill of anticipation in the days between breaking up from school and the wonders of Christmas Day. I recall the ghost of those feelings despite the current situation, despite the reason why Mum and I are here with Angie and Chris instead of spending Christmas together, just the two of us at Mum's, like we usually do. It was Chris who rang to suggest that Mum and I join them this year, largely to take the pressure off me. I like to think that he and Angie discussed it, and that Angie was in agreement, if not

ALBION FAY

the idea's originator, but I'm not convinced and I'm certainly not going to pursue the matter. Angie's mood since Mum and I got here has been, if not frosty, then certainly distant.

Not that that's unusual. As far as I'm aware my sister's problems are ongoing. We don't discuss it, so I'm not certain whether she's still seeing a therapist, but there's no avoiding the many and various bottles of pills in the bathroom cabinet.

For once, though, it's not Angie's mental health that's uppermost in my mind, it's Mum's. With hindsight I see that there were signs of it last Christmas. I had to rush out on Christmas Eve to buy stuffing and cranberry sauce and sprouts because Mum had forgotten them all, and (eschewing tradition) I had to take over the cooking of the Christmas dinner the next day because she was getting too flustered.

But despite Mum's distress at being unable to cope, I didn't think too much of it at the time. I just put it down to the onset of age, and to the fact that — quite understandably — she wasn't as energetic or as on-the-ball as she used to be. Christmas is a big venture, after all. Even when there's just the two of us there's lots to remember. I reassured myself that at least she was still sharp enough to do crosswords and have conversations and answer a lot of the questions on the quiz shows she liked to watch on TV. And she seemed to have no trouble remembering people and events from her past, and the names of her neighbours, and details from articles she'd read in magazines or in the newspaper.

But then gradually, over the next few months, things began to get worse. She started to get absent-minded. She'd forget the names of the most ordinary of objects — the kettle (on one occasion she told me to 'put the cuttlefish on'), the TV, her slippers, the vacuum cleaner. Sometimes she forgot my name too. Now and again she'd drift in the middle of a conversation and stare into space as though she'd been switched off. She became a liability in the kitchen. One time she put an egg on to boil and forgot about it, and it was only the intervention of her next-door neighbor, Kimberley, who saw black smoke pouring from the kitchen window, that prevented the house from burning down.

That was when I started to visit her more regularly. And Kimberley would pop in at least once a day too, to make sure she was all right. It's been a bind these past six months, what with school and everything, but Mum is stubborn and she still has enough about her to get upset at the thought of having to leave her little home because she can no longer take care of herself. Chris's suggestion that we all spend Christmas together this year saved me from a conversation I'd been dreading. If I'd proposed to Mum that she spend Christmas with me, rather than the other way round, she'd have known right away that my reason for asking her was because I thought her no longer capable of hosting our annual celebration. But a proper family Christmas was something else entirely. It was a novelty, a precedent. And what grandparent could resist the prospect of seeing their grandchildren open their presents on Christmas Day?

It's almost midnight now and the house is quiet. Rain is a ceaseless muffled whispering at the windows beyond the thick curtains, and the fire that Chris built earlier has slumped to glowing embers, which still give off more than enough heat to keep us warm.

Angie is on one side of the fire, curled up in an armchair in a shapeless green jumper and long, wooly, multi-coloured socks, and I'm on the other. Because it's Christmas we've drunk more

than usual — wine at dinner and then port afterwards, most of a
bottle of which we've now polished off between us.

I'm feeling mellow. My thoughts are woozy and slow and
my body feels somnolent and oddly pliable, like toffee. I almost
snigger at the image, but to make a sound would involve too much
effort and so I merely smile. Opposite me Angie stares into the
fire with wide, vacant eyes as though hypnotized by the pulse of
orange heat.

She seems so deep within herself that I'm surprised when she
says, "What are we going to do with Mum?"

I lick my lips and try to form my thoughts into a coherent shape.
Finally I say, "I don't know. But she can't go on like she is. Pretty
soon she's going to need round-the-clock care."

Angie sighs and nods, as if to say: *who would have thought,
when we were kids, that it would eventually come to this?* I wonder
if that's what she *is* thinking. It's so difficult to tell these days.

"A home, you mean?" she says.

I shrug. "Maybe. We'll have to look into the possibilities as soon
as Christmas is over."

She lifts her eyes from the fire, though some of its heat seems
to remain in her sockets, the contents of which pulse and flicker.
"Together?"

"If that's what you want," I say carefully.

She nods. "I do."

I'm still cradling my half-full glass, which I lift to my lips.

"Do you think Dad is anything to do with how Mum is now?"
Angie asks.

I swallow a sip of sweet port before answering. "How do you
mean?"

"What he did to her. All those times he hit her. Perhaps he gave her brain damage."

I shake my head. "I doubt it."

"But we can't know for sure, can we? We don't *know* that all those punches didn't have a long term effect?"

"No," I concede. "I suppose we don't."

We fall silent for a moment. I look into the fire. I'm troubled — and I assume Angie is too — by the notion that Mum never escaped from Dad's violence. Then Angie shocks me by saying, "Sometimes I get terrified that Chris will turn out like Dad."

When I look at her, her face gives nothing away. It's so blank that I'm reminded of that time in the hospital when she was ten, the day after she got lost in the cave. Though her comment is not even remotely amusing, I bark a half-laugh and say, "You can't seriously think that?"

She shrugs. "Dad didn't start hitting Mum until we were... what? Ten? Eleven? They must have loved each other once. *He* must have loved *her.*"

I shake my head. "Dad and Chris are two completely different people. Dad was always a... a macho bully. Chris isn't like that. He's a lovely guy, kind and gentle and patient. He's a great husband and a brilliant dad. Anyone can see that."

She doesn't deny it, but neither does she concede the fact. She just looks at me and says, "Did I make them hate each other? Mum and Dad, I mean?"

I don't know how to answer that. I shake my head slowly. Finally I say, "You mean 'we', don't you?"

She nods almost eagerly. "Yes," she says. "We."

When I come downstairs the morning after they let Angie out of the hospital I'm surprised and a little disappointed to find that Mum and Dad are already up. Dad's slumped at the table where we eat our meals, scowling into a cup of coffee, while Mum is drying and putting away the dinner things that have been soaking in the basin overnight. Because we're on holiday and Dad doesn't have to go to work, they usually have a lie-in until at least 8:30, which means I get to read for an hour in peace. Today, though, I hastily stuff my book into the pocket of my dressing gown before Dad can see it. It's only just out of sight when he looks up.

His eyes are baggy and bloodshot and his unshaven face looks greasy and grey.

"Thought you'd finally honour us with your presence, did you?" he mutters.

I'm confused. What does he mean? It's only 7:30. Before I can formulate an answer, Mum turns from the cupboard she's just slammed shut after putting away a stack of pudding bowls and says, "That's unfair, George. Just because we were kept awake doesn't mean that Frank should be."

Dad grunts at her and goes back to his coffee. I look at Mum questioningly. "What's happened?"

She tries to arrange her face into a reassuring expression. "Nothing's *happened*. It's just Angie. She's had a restless night."

"That's a bloody understatement," growls Dad.

Mum flashes him a look. To me she explains, "She had bad dreams. She was upset, calling out in her sleep-"

"Screaming her bloody head off, more like," Dad interrupts.

"She made a right fucking row. If you didn't hear it you must be bloody deaf."

"I didn't," I admit.

"Perhaps we should send you to get your bloody ears cleaned out then."

"George," Mum says sharply, "this isn't helping."

Dad glares at her. His eyes have a strange glitter to them that makes me go cold at the base of my scalp. "Oh, well, I'm sorry if I'm not fucking *helping*," he says.

"And there's no need for bad language. Our Frank doesn't need to hear that."

"I'm sure he hears a lot worse in the playground," says Dad. "Probably swears like a trooper when he's with his mates. All kids do."

"I'm sure he doesn't," Mum says. "Not all children are like you were."

"More's the pity," Dad mutters, staring at me.

His scrutiny makes me want to squirm, but I try not to show how uncomfortable I feel. "What was Angie dreaming about?" I ask Mum.

"She didn't say. I'm not sure she *could* say. She was very confused." She pauses, then adds, "She was sleepwalking too. That's the main reason me and your Dad didn't get much sleep."

Dad's silent for the time being, but his hostility is like heat from a fire, pulsing from him in waves.

"She wanted to get out," Mum continues. "She kept saying she had to go back to the caves. She got quite upset about it."

Silently she rolls up the sleeve of her silk dressing gown and shows me her arm. There are angry-looking scratches on it, deep enough to have drawn blood.

"Did Angie do that?" I ask, shocked.

Mum nods and her eyes glisten with tears. I sense she's suddenly too upset to speak.

"We should have opened the bloody door and let her go," Dad says.

Mum gasps, and though her eyes shimmer, she looks furious. "You don't mean that!"

"Don't I?" says Dad. "At least then we'd have been able to get a decent night's sleep."

Even though a tear overspills her lower right eyelid and trickles down her cheek, Mum's face contorts in fury. "My God, you're such a pig!"

Whatever Dad's response might have been is postponed by the opening of the kitchen door. We all turn to see Angie standing there. At first I think she's sleepwalking again. Her eyes are wide and unblinking and her expression is as blank as when I saw her in the hospital. Then she asks dreamily, "What's going on?"

Mum glances warningly at Dad and offers Angie a tight smile. "Nothing, sweetheart. We were just talking."

"I heard shouting. You sounded angry."

Instead of providing an explanation, Mum says, "How are *you* this morning? Do you want some breakfast?"

Angie frowns slightly, as if Mum's questions are a puzzle she can't fathom, and in the pause during which we wait for an answer, I suddenly realize what it is about Angie's appearance that strikes me as odd.

It isn't just that she's wearing her clothes over her pyjamas, which poke out from underneath, it's that she's turned her clothes inside out. The tufted inner seams of her jumper and jeans are on the outside, and the jeans' pockets are like two little white holsters on her hips.

Dad seems to register this at the same time as I do, and his eyes blaze with anger, as though Angie is doing this to goad him. "What the fuck is this shit now? Are you bloody simple?"

"George!" Mum snaps, but he ignores her.

"Go and get dressed properly." When Angie doesn't move he bellows, "*Now!*"

I jump at the sudden volume of his voice, but Angie doesn't even flinch. She stands her ground and shakes her head slowly.

"I can't."

Dad stands up so suddenly that his thighs bump the edge of the table, shifting it a few screeching inches across the floor. "Don't 'can't' me, girl. You'll do what I bloody well tell you."

But Angie still shakes her head. "They'll come if I do."

Mum raises a hand towards Dad like a traffic policeman, but her attention is focused on Angie. "Who'll come, sweetheart?"

Now Angie looks fearful. Her eyes flicker briefly to the windows and her voice drops to a whisper. "The Fay."

"What the bloody hell are you talking about?" Dad snarls.

Mum's head snaps round, her expression changing from gentleness to anger. "Will you shut up, George. You're not helping."

Dad darts round the side of the table so quickly that I stumble and almost fall as I take an instinctive step back.

"I'm bloody fed up of this," he says and stalks towards Angie.

Mum steps into his path. "You leave her alone."

"Get out of my way," snaps Dad. "She needs bloody sorting out."

"Oh, and what are you going to do? Knock some sense into her?"

"If I have to."

"You're not going to lay a finger-"

And that's when Dad swings a fist round and wallops Mum on the side of the head.

I'm so shocked that for an instant everything seems to stop. It's as if the impossible has happened, as if some major, unbreakable rule of the universe has just been shattered.

But of course nothing stops really. Mum is knocked sideways with such force that she falls down. It's horrible. Grown-ups aren't supposed to fall over like children, but she collapses like her bones have disappeared out of her legs. What makes it worse is that the kitchen is so narrow that as she goes down she hits her head on the door of the cupboard underneath the sink. It makes an awful crack, like two boulders colliding. For a moment I'm convinced her skull will break into pieces like a dropped pot.

It doesn't, though. There's not even any blood, not at first anyway. When Mum stops falling, when she's just lying there, I expect her to start crying, but instead she makes wheezy, high-pitched gasping sounds like she can't breathe properly, which is even worse.

I'm so stunned I can't move, can't even speak, but Angie can. She steps towards Dad, even though he reminds me of a werewolf, the way he's standing with his fists still clenched and his shoulders rising and falling as he breathes heavily in and out. Looking up at him Angie says, "Now look what you've done."

I think Dad's going to roar like an animal and fly at her. I think he's going to tear her to pieces, and I wonder what I'll do if that happens.

But it doesn't. Dad stares back at Angie for a moment and then his gaze flickers away. He looks at Mum on the floor. He looks at me. He says, "Sod the lot of you." Then he turns and walks out of the house.

*

Angie has got it into her head that she needs to see Scott again. Or rather, that she needs to see Scott's grandmother, though to do that she first has to find Scott. The problem is we don't know where Scott lives or even what his second name is. We didn't arrange to see the boys again when we said goodbye to them the other day. Personally I was so relieved to have survived an encounter with a group of older boys unscathed that it didn't even occur to me to suggest keeping in touch. Now, though, Angie has decided it's crucial she finds out everything that Scott's grandmother knows about the Fay. But the only way of maybe meeting Scott again that she can think of is to go back to the ruins of the factory in the woods in the hope that he'll turn up.

"Maybe the boys go there all the time," she says.

I think it's a dumb idea, but Angie is so adamant to give it a try that she says she'll go alone if needs be. Of course, that's out of the question. Mum will only let us out of the house from now on if we stick together. Even if *she* didn't insist on it, *I* would; I've become terrified of losing my sister. Despite the sunshine that wakes us up each morning and illuminates the majority of each day here, I can't help feeling that there's a shadow hanging over us, an evil 'something' that, having tasted Angie's soul, now wants it for good.

Maybe that's just me being stupid, but it still doesn't help to shake off my notion that Angie's at risk and vulnerable. I feel on tenterhooks, as if we're being constantly watched, which is a different feeling to the fear I have that Dad will hit Mum again. What makes my anxiety worse is that secretly I think there's a part of Angie that *wants* to disappear. It's as if the 'something' planted a seed inside her brain when she was in the cave and every so often it calls to her and she feels an overwhelming desire to go to it. I'm glad that today is Thursday, and that in two days time we'll be going home. Maybe, away from this place, the influence of the 'something' will weaken and die. I hope so.

For now, though, I'm determined to watch Angie like a hawk, and to protect her if needs be. Of course, if the 'something' were actually to come for her, I'm not sure what I'd do. I like to think I'd stand and fight, but maybe I'd just panic and run. Of course, I tell myself a hundred times a day, nothing *is* going to happen. There's no such thing as the Fay. My fears all come from my own imagination.

If Angie had her way she'd be wearing her clothes inside out again, but even Mum, who's been patient and understanding with her since she re-emerged from the caves, has put her foot down this time. She hasn't lost her temper, though, like Dad did and like I sometimes feel like doing. She's been kind and gentle, but she's told Angie that if she insists on wearing her clothes like that, then it means Angie isn't yet well enough to go outside and has to stay where Mum can keep an eye on her.

Angie tried to argue, but Mum stood firm, and in the end Angie nodded and agreed with Mum that she was being silly and unreasonable. So she went upstairs to change and came down wearing her T-shirt and jeans the proper way. But once we descend the steps to the bottom of the garden and cross the road and are in the woods, Angie confesses to me that when she went upstairs she turned her knickers and socks inside out. Worriedly she looks around as she tells me this, though there's nothing to see but a thick, minutely shifting mass of trees and bushes.

"I hope it's enough," she says.

"Enough for what?" I ask her.

"Enough to keep them away."

Her words unsettle me, which makes me tetchy. "If you're so scared of them, why don't we just go back and stay in the house until it's time to go home?"

She looks at me like I'm mad. "I can't do that."

She doesn't explain why and I don't ask her. We walk the rest of the way in silence and reach the ruins without incident. They haven't changed since the last time we were here; the only thing that has is Angie. She looks smaller somehow; she's less confident, less inclined to draw attention to herself. As soon as we tramp down the muddy hill and are among the ruins proper, she says, "Wait a minute," and peels off her T-shirt.

She's only ten, so she hasn't got boobs yet, but her chest is definitely changing. Her nipples aren't flat like they used to be; they stand out from her skin, and they look softer somehow, as if they would feel like velvet if you touched them. It makes me feel weird to look at them, so I turn away and pretend to be interested in the crumbling structures around me. I hear her scuffling about for a bit and when I eventually turn back her T-shirt and jeans are inside-out again.

"*Why* does it keep them away?" I ask.

She shrugs. "I don't know. It just does."

"But how do you know?"

Her eyes are glassy. "I just do."

I sigh deeply. When it comes to the Fay, Angie is like a wall that my questions keep bouncing back from. "So what do we do now?"

"We wait. What did Mum give us to eat this time?"

I shrug the rucksack I've been carrying off my back and hand it to her. "Have a look for yourself. I'm not really hungry."

As Angie opens the rucksack and roots around inside I walk about, looking up at the rim of the 'bowl' that encircles us. The point where the earth ends and the sky begins is a hazy space, light and dark bleeding into one another. It makes me feel that reality isn't quite solid up there, that by stepping over the brink Angie and I have passed from one realm to another. Perhaps the same rules don't apply down here, I think, perhaps the magic of the Fay is stronger among the ruins. Is that why it feels constantly damp down here, why there's an odour of mulchy decay?

I shiver and eventually turn away. Angie is sitting on a portion of low wall beside a tree whose half-exposed roots have prised up part of the structure and caused dark splits to zigzag through the brickwork. She has the rucksack between her feet and she is munching on a sausage roll, flakes of pastry sticking to her bottom lip. Seeing her like that, slightly hunched over, I feel so protective that I get a fierce urge to go across and put my arm around her. So I do. I walk over, sit down beside her and drape an arm across her shoulders. She looks at me and smiles.

"Do you want a sausage roll? They're really nice."

"Go on then."

We munch sausage rolls together. The only sound is a slight whispering above us that doesn't mean we're being spied on, just that a breeze is ruffling the highest leaves in the trees. Even so, I glance up nervously now and again, expecting to see dark figures up on the rim ducking away out of sight.

"What are we going to do about Mum and Dad?" Angie says.

Her question makes the mouthful of chewed pastry and sausage meat in my mouth hard to swallow. I force it down and say cautiously, "What do you mean?"

Her answer comes back immediately and fiercely. "He's hit her twice now. Maybe more. He's not going to stop."

The food I've eaten seems to crawl in my belly. "Maybe he will when we get home. Maybe it's just this place that's making him do it."

The way she's looking at me makes me feel ashamed of offering excuses for him. "Do you really think that?"

I shrug. "I don't know."

"Well, *I* do. He *won't* stop. He's a big fat bully. Now he knows he *can* do it he'll *keep* doing it."

I think about what she's said and it frightens me. The thought of Mum being hit on a regular basis is unbearable.

"What can *we* do?" I say. "We're just kids."

"If he does it again we'll have to tell someone."

"Who?"

For a moment she looks uncertain, then she says, "The police."

I'm shocked. "We can't tell the police about our own dad."

"Why not?" she snaps.

"Well... we just can't. He's our dad."

"So? He's a shitty dad."

"Angie!" I say, horrified.

She looks flushed, as if she's been caught doing something she shouldn't, but her eyes flash with defiance. "Well, he *is* shitty. He's always saying horrible things to us. I hate him."

I look quickly around, as if terrified he might be somewhere close by, listening. In a hushed voice, I say, "You can't say that."

"Why not?" she says again.

"You just *can't*."

I have a vague idea that saying bad things about your parents, whatever you may think of them, is a bit like saying bad things about God. It's blasphemy. And blasphemers, so our headmaster, Mr Coleman tells us, always get punished. Once again I glance up to where the rising slope meets the painfully bright sky, half-expecting to see... what? A black cloud full of lightning bolts? A horde of avenging angels?

Or maybe the Fay, which — despite my dream on the night of Angie's disappearance — I now imagine to be black and spindly and twisted, like creatures made of roots and twigs and thorns. I picture them gathering up on the hillside, a dark, spiky mass, like a thicket of brambles come to life. So strong is this image that for a split-second I actually see them and rise to my feet in alarm. But then Angie says, "What's the matter?" and when I look again all I see is mud and grass and shadows enfolded within tangled clumps of foliage.

"Nothing," I say, and start to sit down again.

But I've only just begun to bend my knees when we hear a noise.

It comes from somewhere near the big chimney, which is about the distance of two football pitches behind us. I jump up again and whirl round, and Angie too rises, though more slowly than I do.

By the time we're staring at the place where the noise seemed to come from it's already stopped. I'm certain, though, that what we both heard was a tumble of bricks, as if the remains of a wall had collapsed or been pushed over. I could tell they were bricks and not stones because of the flinty clatter they made. There's no evidence of where they might have come from, though. No fresh piles of rubble, no settling cloud of dust.

Angie and I look at each other, then Angie calls, "Hello?"

There's no answer.

After a few seconds she adds, "Anyone there?"

Between us and the chimney is a flat, wide area of rubble-strewn mud, knobbly with embedded stones and roots. At the far end of this is a small banking, straggly with weedy undergrowth, that dips down to a lower level. Flanking both sides of this passage or walkway are the skeletal ruins of the factory and its various outbuildings, which mostly consist of a collection of unsupported walls of varying heights, round and within which the forest has grown.

"Maybe it was just another bit of the factory falling down, " I say, gesturing vaguely beyond those walls that are visible to us.

"Or maybe we're being watched," Angie replies.

Before I can tell her to be careful, she's walking towards the walkway's edge where the banking dips down to the hollow from which the chimney rises. I jog a few paces and then fall into step beside her, feeling as though the walls are pressing in on either side of us, even though this passageway would be wide enough to accommodate a delivery lorry with room to spare — provided you could get one through the woods and down the banking. My head turns from side to side as I scan the ruins, imagining black, spiny shapes keeping pace with us, using the surrounding walls as cover. I don't hear anything, but that's no comfort. Perhaps the Fay move silently. Perhaps they have wings. Perhaps they're as weightless as ghosts.

Then Angie interrupts my train of thought with a sharp gasp.

My head snaps round to face front. At first I think a portion of the banking beyond the slope is bulging towards us. I imagine a mole (though it would have to be a large one, possibly even the size of a man) tunneling upwards, the earth swelling as it rises towards the surface. Then my vision adjusts as something heaves itself over the edge of the walkway and scrambles to its feet and I realize it's a large black dog.

Instantly my heart accelerates and I feel a slackening in my gut, as though fear is causing something to uncoil in there. My hand shoots out and I grab Angie's arm tightly enough to make her hiss in pain, perhaps even to leave bruises. There's a low, flat buzzing in my ears, which I associate with the heat. My throat tightens like a sphincter.

I think: *It's all real. Everything Scott told us is real.*

The dog raises its head and looks at us. It sniffs the air cautiously. I don't know what sort of dog it is, some kind of mastiff, I think. Though large, its sleek, coal-black body is solid and compact, its chest so wide it looks almost bow-legged. It has froth on its jowls, but it does not appear hostile. It regards us steadily.

Its eyes are not red, though, and this gives me hope. Hope that we still inhabit the world that Angie and I know and understand. Our world is one of rules and certainties, one where the ground is solid and time flows at a steady, even pace. A world where magic does not exist. A world in which there is nothing that can't be explained, nothing that hasn't been discovered.

I tell myself this, but do I really believe it?

More to the point, just because our world is real does that automatically make it *safe*? I'm pretty sure I know the answer to that one.

The dog is still regarding us and we are still standing side by side staring at it. I incline my head towards Angie, slowly so as not to antagonize it, and whisper, "Who do you think it belongs to?"

She looks at me in such a way that for an instant I'm convinced she's about to say, 'It doesn't belong to anybody'. But she doesn't say that. She doesn't say anything. She simply reaches across with her left hand and prises my grip from her right arm. As my fingers come free I see the red marks I've made and feel shocked and ashamed. I want to say sorry, but she doesn't seem to feel any pain. She reaches up and places a hand silently on my chest in a gesture whose meaning is obvious: *Stay here.*

No, I start to say, *don't*, but the expression on her face freezes me. I stand, as if rendered immobile, as she breaks away and walks slowly forward. The dog watches her advance implacably. It doesn't move. I wonder, if it suddenly attacked, how long it would take me to scoop up a loose brick — there are plenty lying around — and throw it (*probably too long*), and whether, even if I managed to hit my target, it would be enough to distract the dog or even frighten it away (*probably not*).

Angie takes slow, measured paces until she's maybe ten metres from the dog, which still hasn't moved, and then she stops. She and the dog look at each other with such intent that I wonder if they're communicating telepathically. Eventually Angie leans forward slightly from the waist and does something I've never seen her do before: she spits on the ground. Then, in a low, determined voice, she says, "Go back to where you came from."

The dog raises its head slightly and gives the barest twitch of its ears, as if snatching her words from the air.

Slowly Angie raises a hand and points at it.

"Go back to where you came from," she repeats. "I'm not coming with you." And then, in little more than a murmur, she adds something that sends a chill through me despite the heat of the day: "Not yet."

The dog raises its head once more and sniffs the air. Foam drips from its jowls. I get the feeling that it's making an assessment, coming to a decision. Angie's body is rigid, her hand still upraised.

And then, with no further ceremony, the dog turns, the movement lithe and quick despite its bulk, and slips away, disappearing back over the edge of the slope. As soon as it's gone Angie starts to sway, as if she's about to faint. I rush forward to catch her before she can fall.

As soon as I put my arms around her, she turns her head and offers me a faint smile. She looks tired and pale, like someone convalescing from a long illness who has tried to do too much too soon.

"Are you all right?" I ask in a breathless rush. And then, glancing at the empty space where seconds before the dog had been standing, "Was that... one of them?"

The look she gives me is what I can only describe as an 'old' look. It is the look of someone who has seen far more than she can possibly explain, especially to someone as young and inexperienced as me. I have to remind myself that she is my twin sister, that we are the same age, that we have shared almost the same experiences.

Her voice, however, is a dry rasp. It sounds like the voice of someone much older than she is.

"Let's go home," she says.

*

I put the oldest of the photograph albums aside, placing it almost reverently on the settee beside me, and lift the next one out of the box. I take a deep, shuddering breath and then I open the stiff, leather-look cover. The creak it makes as I fold it back is like the tiniest of whimpers. The first photograph I see is of Angie, tired, washed-out, but smiling, lying in a hospital bed, holding two-day-old Aspen in her arms.

It's almost immediately after I take this photograph that Angie asks me if I'd like to hold Aspen. I'm nervous, but I lift my new niece carefully, almost reverently, into the crook of my arm. I'm amazed at how light she is, and I marvel at her tiny but perfectly formed fists. I gently stroke one of those fists with the tip of my little finger and the fist responds as if independent of its owner. The fingers open out like the fronds of some delicate undersea plant and wrap themselves tightly around my finger. I grin at Angie and say, "She's got quite a grip on her!" as if this is something to be celebrated, and Angie nods indulgently. I lean forward and kiss Aspen's forehead, breathing in her milky smell, and feel a stab of alarm at how her fontanelle pulses, at how vulnerable she is.

This is my first memory of Aspen, and it wrenches an involuntary sob from me. Immediately I snap the book shut as if I can trap that moment in its pages, preserve it for ever. If only it was that easy. If only particular moments could be re-lived and particular memories extracted like teeth. The memory I would most like expunged is less than a month old, and yet I'm already certain it has become my own personal ghost, one that will haunt me for ever.

It is Chris's PA Valerie who calls me. She wants to know why Chris hasn't been at work for three days, why he isn't answering his phone or replying to his emails.

"Is something the matter?" she asks.

"Not that I know of," I say, feeling resentful and irritable. I don't tell her that I have problems of my own, that I am facing a criminal investigation because a spiteful thirteen-year-old called Tamsin Wicks has accused me of assaulting her.

I haven't assaulted her, of course. All I've done is march across to her desk during a lesson, grab her arms and force them down to her sides. I've done this because, despite numerous warnings, she kept raising her arms and putting her hands on her head, which meant that the pupils behind her were unable to see the blackboard.

"That's assault, that is!" she bleats at me. "You're not supposed to touch me! You're a fucking pervert, sir! I'm fucking reporting you!"

Part of me is amused that she still calls me 'sir' while accusing me of being a 'fucking pervert'. I sigh as though she's being tiresome, which she is, and say, "Don't be ridiculous, Tamsin."

But she does report me. And what's more, I'm suspended pending an inquiry. Sue Glasson, the head, says she has no alternative. She says she's doing it with regret.

I turn my attention back to Valerie, who is still talking.

"Well, it's not like him," Valerie is saying. "He's usually so reliable. I'm getting a bit worried."

"I'm sure everything's fine," I assure her.

But Valerie is on a roll now and doesn't seem to hear me. "I mean, if he was ill he'd have called in sick, or Angie would. I mean, he would have, wouldn't he?"

This time she pauses to hear my answer. I say, "Perhaps Angie's sick too. Perhaps they've got a virus or something. Or perhaps they've been called away unexpectedly."

Then it strikes me. Valerie is right. Nothing would stop Chris from letting people know if something was wrong. He is Mr Reliable, Mr Responsibility. Having been with my sister for twenty five years he has *had* to be.

I feel a quiver deep in my gut. It isn't presentiment, nothing like that, it's just nervous anxiety. Perfectly natural, given the circumstances.

Before Valerie can respond to my previous suggestion I say, "Have you been to the house?"

"Not yet," she says. "I was thinking of going today. Do you want to meet me there after work?"

I can tell by her voice that she's asking me because she's afraid of what she might find. I say, "No need, I'll go round there now." I feel compelled to add, "I've got a day off."

Twenty minutes later the house comes into view as I round the final corner at the end of the cul-de-sac. I'm not sure what I expect to see, but I'm relieved that everything appears fine. I'm even more relieved that the family Renault — Angie and Chris only have one car — is not parked in the driveway.

There you are then, I think. *They've gone away.* An entire scenario plays out in my head in the few seconds that it takes me to park at the kerb and turn the engine off: an impromptu holiday, somewhere remote with no phone signal and no internet. I even picture Chris saying, *I ought to let them know at work*, and Angie replying, *Oh, why live by the rules all the time? Come on, Chris. Let's just go!*

I can imagine that of the old Angie, the cheeky, skinny, vivacious ten-year-old girl that she once was, but what of the wizened, joyless, frightened creature she has now become? The image evaporates as I get out of the car and close the door. As I look up at the house — curtains open, everything neat and tidy — and then start walking towards it, the quiver of anxiety in my belly becomes a judder and I clench my fist around the keys in my hand.

By the time I reach the front door I'm trembling so badly that it takes me several tries before I manage to slide the key into the lock. *Come on*, I say to myself, *this is ridiculous*. And then I push the door open and the smell hits me.

I recoil, but in truth it's not as strong as it first seems. Its initial pungency is only due to the fact that I've been outside in the fresh air and that the house has been shut up for several days. After a few seconds the smell — which makes me think of a pig farm — partially dissipates. Even so, I'm shaking like crazy, and breathing so fast that my head is swimming. My mouth is so dry it feels full of blotting paper.

I consider calling the police, but what if the smell is just rotting food? Would they think I was wasting their time? Would they give me the look Dad always used to give me, the one that made it clear he thought I was a 'puff', a 'cissy', a 'nancy boy'? Even after all these years I'm not sure I could stand that. And so, leaving the front door open to get as much air as possible, I step further into the house.

Even though my throat is dry, I manage, after several attempts, to croak out a greeting. "Angie? Chris? Anyone home?"

There is no response. I stand for a moment, wondering which way to go. Directly ahead of me across the small, square hallway is a staircase, which branches both left and right at the top. To my left is a door which leads into the front room, at the back of which another door leads into a dining room. To my right is what Chris jokingly calls the 'music room' where the girls practice their instruments of choice — there's a piano in there for Aspen and a music stand which nine year old India uses when she plays her clarinet. The music room leads into the kitchen, which in turn leads out in to the back garden and also into the dining room through a side door.

Because the rooms are all inter-connected around the central staircase, I could turn either left or right here and pass from one room to another until I'm back at my starting point. I hesitate for several seconds longer, until I reach the stage where I think that if I don't make a decision imminently I never will, and then my left hand darts out and grabs the handle of the door into the front room and I push it open.

This time the smell that assails me is so thickly rancid that it seems to haze the air like smoke. I choke and gag and reel back, my eyes watering. I press a hand to my mouth, but it barely helps; my skin already seems impregnated with the stench. I wish that instead of marching directly to the front door from my car I had taken an extra few seconds to step off the drive, walk across the lawn and peer into this room through the big picture window that looks out on to the hedge-bordered front garden.

For a moment I consider pulling the door closed and doing just that, but I can't face the prospect of dragging this wretched ordeal out any longer. And so, my hand wrapped tightly around the doorknob (I feel a need for something solid to cling to) I shove the door open another half-metre or so and step smartly into the room.

Chris is sprawled on the sofa, but he's barely recognizable. After three days, which is how long I assume he's been dead judging by the last time he was at work, his skin has become discoloured and his decomposing body has begun to bloat. I look at him for less than a second (though the split-second image is burned on to my retina and, I suspect, will never leave me) before exiting the room, dragging the door shut as I do so. My mind seems unable to respond to what I've just seen, though my body does so instinctively. As I wheel away from the now-closed door I raise my right hand to my mouth, but succeed only in puking through my fingers.

I throw up twice more on the wooden floor of the hallway, my body bent almost double. Afterwards my stomach and throat feel as though they've been scoured with sandpaper. I don't realize I'm sobbing until I hear myself, at which point I drag a handkerchief out of my pocket and use it to dry the tears on my face and wipe the puke off my hand.

On shaking legs I check the music room, the kitchen and the dining room, but they're all empty. I don't want to go upstairs, but I know that I have to. I could call the police and wait for them on the drive, but it would take them at least ten minutes, maybe more, to arrive and check out the house and I don't think I could endure that period of not-knowing. I ascend the stairs almost like a toddler, hauling my weak and trembling body up by clawing at the steps above me. The same stench that hit me when I opened the door of the front room thickens again as I get closer to the top, and by the time I reach the landing I'm gagging once again, though there's nothing to bring up this time.

I find Aspen and India in their beds, tucked up as though for a night's sleep. Like Chris, their skin is a livid purple-red and their faces are hideous, bloated Halloween masks, their mouths yawning open. India's duvet, which is cream with a pink butterfly design on it, is stained with some dark, brownish fluid that I assume are the evacuated contents of her bladder and bowels.

wI want to scream, but I can't; it is as if a hand is clutching me tightly around the throat.

I don't find Angie's body. I search the rest of the house, but there's no sign of her. I think of her dead husband and children, and the fact that the car is gone, but I can't, I refuse, to make further connections. I stagger downstairs, and outside in the street, halfway to my car, I collapse in the road. I'm sweating and shaking and crying. I feel ill, as though my body is running with fever. I can't see or think straight. My mind is a blur. It is only later that I discover it was a neighbor who found me and called the police. Even now I remember the rest of the afternoon only in snippets and shards: my face pressed against the gritty pavement as my empty stomach convulses; sipping tea in an unfamiliar house, my teeth chattering against the rim of a red mug; sitting in the back of a police car that smells of lemon-scented air freshener, a blanket around my shoulders and a female police officer with a cold sore on her upper lip speaking to me gently.

The post mortem, several days later, reveals that Chris, Aspen and India died from ingesting a lethal cocktail of poisonous substances which had almost certainly been added to their last meal. The cocktail contained massive doses of cyanide, heroin and nimetazepam, the latter of which was in the form of dozens of crushed-up sleeping tablets.

"Their killer clearly wanted them to suffer as little as possible," I'm told by Detective Inspector Sherman, who is leading the murder inquiry, and who interviews me a day after the post mortem findings. "Although their deaths weren't pleasant they would have lapsed into unconsciousness very quickly, possibly within seconds once the poisons started to take effect." He leans forward across the table in the interview room, the fingers of his hands laced together. Although his manner is business-like, his eyes and voice are full of sympathy.

"Can you think of any reason why your sister, Angharad, would want to kill her family, Mr Ryan?"

In the few days since finding the bodies I have thought of nothing else and I tell DI Sherman of a conversation I had with Angie not long ago, possibly the last proper conversation I had with her.

"She told me that she was scared her family would be taken away from her," I say.

He frowns. "Taken away how? By death, you mean?"

I shake my head. "When we were kids something happened to Angie. She went into some caves one day and got lost. She was missing for hours. When she found her way out again she was... different."

"Different how?" the Inspector asks.

"It's like she was... haunted. Or marked maybe. Yes, that's probably closer to it. She thought there were... creatures after her. Creatures that somehow had claim to her. She called them the Fay."

"So you're saying your sister thought these creatures would one day come back and... what? Take her family away?"

I nod. "I think Angie thought she'd eventually be punished for not going with them when she was supposed to. I think she thought the Fay would take her family to teach her a lesson. And so, to prevent that happening..."

"She killed them," says the Inspector.

"Yes," I say. "What she did wasn't a cruel act or an evil one. It was an act of kindness. She killed Chris and the girls because she thought she was saving them from a worse fate. She did it out of love."

*

We're in a place called a refuge. It's like a sort of hotel for ladies who have left their husbands like Mum. Some of the ladies have kids or babies and some don't. Some of the ladies seem scared, and never want to go out, and cry a lot, and there's one lady, Mrs Booth, who has red wrinkled skin down one side of her face and a milky white eye that she sometimes covers with an eye patch. A lot of the younger kids are scared of her, and I have to admit I'm quite nervous too at first, but it turns out she's really kind. Mum tells me she looks like she does because her husband blinded her with boiling water from a kettle.

"Are all husbands like that, Mum?" I ask, concerned. I have a notion that perhaps there's something about getting married that turns a man from nice to nasty, from mild-mannered to violent.

I'm sitting up in the double bed I've been sharing with Angie for the past few weeks, a book in my hands. The bed's lumpy and old and it creaks whenever Angie or me turn over in it, but it's fun sharing a room with Angie and Mum, who sleeps in a bed on her own against the opposite wall.

Mum has just washed her hair in the communal bathroom down the corridor and it's all wrapped up in a turban that she's made out of a towel. She's wearing a fluffy white dressing gown and equally fluffy slippers, which she bought from Marks and Spencer not long after we moved in here because the house, with its high ceilings and wooden floors and old-fashioned radiators, is quite cold. She's rubbing white cream into her now-healed face, her slim hands moving deftly, expertly across her cheeks and forehead in perfect unison. She pauses a moment and smiles at me, though she looks a little puzzled.

"What do you mean, Frank?" she asks.

I glance at Angie. She's lying on her side with her back to me, her head propped on one hand. Her other hand is idly flicking over the pages of *Jackie* magazine, which is open on the bed before her.

"Well," I say, a little uncertain, "are they all horrible, like..."

I'm about to say 'Dad', but then I realize and leave the sentence hanging. Even now I feel uncomfortable criticizing my father. Despite what he's done to Mum, it seems... disloyal somehow.

"Like Mrs Booth's husband, you mean?" Mum says, and I nod gratefully.

Mum looks a little sad. She shakes her head. "Not all. Not even most, in fact. The majority of husbands are kind and loving..."

Now *her* voice trails off, and I worry that I've upset her.

"All the ladies *here* seem to have horrible husbands," I say, more to fill the silence than anything.

Next to me Angie tuts. "That's because this is a home for battered wives, dummy."

Mum frowns. "We don't call it that, Angie. It's a refuge, a safe place."

"How long will we have to stay here?" I ask.

"Why?" says Mum. "Don't you like it?"

"No," I say, "it's nice. It's just..." I'm not sure how to continue without sounding ungrateful.

It *is* nice here, and it's fun having loads of other kids to play with, but at the same time I sometimes feel trapped, stifled, as though this is really a prison *disguised* as a hotel. We can't really go out — well, we *could* if we wanted to, but we don't — apart from to school, but even then Mrs Hardy (who insists we call her Linda, which is a bit weird, because she's at least fifty) who runs this place takes us right up to the main doors in the minibus every day, and then picks us up again in the same place at 3:30. Apart from that we just stay here all the time. We don't go for days out, or to the park, or to the shops, and we're not even allowed to stay for any of the after school clubs. I used to go to chess club on Wednesdays, but I don't any more. I know it's because the ladies here are worried that their husbands will get them or their kids while they're out, but it's still annoying. I know what Dad did to Mum, but I can't believe he'd do anything to us in a public place.

All the same, the ladies act as if we're under siege from a pack of wolves. I'm sure some of the husbands they've run away from are even worse than Dad (Mrs Booth's husband, for instance), but it isn't really all that dangerous. In the nearly four weeks we've been here only two of the ladies' husbands have turned up, and both times they just banged on the door and shouted a lot and then the police came and took them away.

Mum smiles at me and nods. "I know," she says. "I know this situation isn't ideal. But it'll only be for a little while, I promise. We'll get our own place soon and then everything will be back to normal."

I wonder how this is going to happen, but I don't ask. Does Mum have any money to buy a new place? She doesn't have a job, so it seems unlikely. And even if we did get a new place, what would stop Dad from coming round and bothering us? Maybe Mum thinks we can go somewhere far away where Dad won't find us, but if we did that how would Mum and Dad get a divorce, and what about all our other stuff at the house we had to leave behind?

Thinking about it makes my head ache. It just seems like a big mess, like a thorny tangle of problems with no solutions. I want to help Mum, but I don't know how. I decide the best thing I can do is not to ask questions and not complain. And so I smile and say, "It's okay, there's no rush. We're fine here for a bit, aren't we, Angie?"

Angie says, "Mmm," but I don't think she's really listening.

I give Mum another smile, a big one this time to show her how happy I am, and then I go back to my book.

When I fall asleep that night I dream that I'm at school and Dad is knocking on the window, but everyone's ignoring him. I'm the only one who seems able to see or hear him, and I feel a terrible dread that even if he were to smash his way in through the window and grab me no one would react, not even the teacher. I try to tell the teacher that he's there, but my throat is paralysed; I can't speak. Dad knocks louder and he's got a terrible grin on his face and his eyes are staring, burning. I try to get up from my desk, only to find that I'm wrapped in a net. I struggle to escape.

And then I wake up.

It's not the end of the dream, though. The knocking has followed me into the real world. I think it's coming from the window, but then Mum snaps on her bedside lamp and the light helps me to orientate myself. I realize the knocking is not coming from the window, but from the opposite side of the room. Someone is banging on the door.

"What is it?" Mum calls, sounding less confused than she looks.

"It's Joyce, Mrs Ryan," says a voice. "Joyce Pallister."

Mum wrinkles her face up as if she's tasted something sour. Mrs Pallister is nosey and a bit of a gossip and I get the feeling that some of the other ladies don't like her very much.

"What is it, Joyce?" Mum says in a voice that suggests she'd better have a good reason for waking us all up.

"It's probably not my place to say," Joyce says, "but I thought you ought to know — your husband's outside."

She says this almost as though it's a good thing, or at least as if she's pleased with herself for telling us. Mum leaps out of bed as if a spider has crawled from under her pillow. I don't realize Angie is awake until she levers herself up on her elbows and says groggily, "Why's Dad here?"

Mum looks scared and angry at the same time. She yanks her dressing gown on as if it's annoyed her in some way.

"Never mind," she snaps. "Go back to sleep."

"Are you going to talk to him?" I ask.

"No," she says, "I'm not."

"How did he know we were here?" asks Angie.

"God knows," Mum says. "You two wait here. I'll see what's going on."

"I want to come," says Angie.

"No!" says Mum. "Stay here with your brother."

From outside the door, Mrs Pallister asks, "Is everything all right in there?"

Mum's head snaps round to glare at the door. "Perfectly, thank you," she barks, "not that it's any business of yours. If you don't mind I'm talking to my children."

Mrs Pallister says, "Charming," and then grumbles something else, but she's moving away from the door now.

"That bloody woman," Mum mutters.

"Will you be all right, Mum?" Angie asks.

The scowl on Mum's face softens into a smile, though it's not a convincing one. "Course I will," she says. "Don't worry, I'll be back in a few minutes."

She steps into her slippers, then crosses the room and goes out of the door.

We hear her feet scuffing down the wooden corridor, growing fainter with each step.

"What do you think Dad wants?" I say to Angie.

She throws back the covers on her side and swings her legs out of bed. "Let's go and see."

"We can't do that!" I say, but Angie is already crossing the room.

She glances back briefly over her shoulder. "Why not?"

"Mum told us to wait here!"

When her face curls into a sneer she reminds me of Dad. "I'm not staying here when Dad's outside. I want to see what he wants."

She's only wearing pyjamas and her feet are bare, but she grabs the door handle and turns it.

"You'll get into trouble with Mum," I say desperately.

She shrugs. "So what? She'll only shout at me a bit. It doesn't bother me."

I want to tell her that's not the point, that the worst thing would be upsetting Mum, but she's already out of the door and padding along the corridor. I swear, but I get out of bed too and hurry after her. I have no intention of staying here on my own, waiting for news.

I catch up to her in the corridor and we hurry silently through the house, passing closed doors behind which people are sleeping. Although all the main lights are off, it's not hard to see where we're going because the ceilings are studded with little orange night-lights. Even though it's late I'm surprised we don't meet anyone as we make our way along one corridor and then another towards the staircase. I know, because Mum has told me, that this place is often a hive of activity right through the night, what with ladies who can't sleep, or who are up feeding their babies, or with little kids having nightmares or going to the toilet.

We're half-way down the big, wide, creaking staircase when we hear the shouting. I know it's Dad because he keeps shouting Mum's name, but I'm shocked at how raw and desperate he sounds.

I come to a halt, clutching the banister. Angie descends another few steps, then stops too and turns to look at me. "What's wrong with you?"

I gape at her. "Can't you hear that?"

"Yeah, so?"

She never used to be this cold before we went to Albion Fay; this is something that's happened in the last couple of years. She isn't like it all the time, but her moods seem more changeable these days. Mum says it's hormones, but I often wonder whether, when Angie finally emerged from the caves that day, she left a vital part of herself behind. Or maybe it's simpler, more brutal than that. Maybe Dad's treatment of Mum these past two years has hardened her.

"He sounds like..." I can't think of anything at first, and then I can "... like a wounded animal."

Angie's face twists into an expression of fierce satisfaction. "Good," she says — almost spitting the word out. "I hope he's really suffering. He deserves to."

He's our dad I want to say, but I don't, because just being our dad doesn't make him deserving of our love and respect and compassion. I know that Angie's right — he *does* deserve to suffer.

I simply don't have that coldness in my heart that she has; I should do, but I don't.

Angie's squinting at me, like she can read all these conflicting thoughts swimming in my head. "You don't feel *sorry* for him, do you?"

I shake my head, perhaps a little too vigorously. "No way."

"Good," she says and abruptly turns away. "Come on then."

We go down the stairs and along another corridor, which opens out into a wide hallway. The big front door, which has been pounded on and kicked plenty by irate husbands, is made of thick oak, and on the inside are lots of big locks and chains.

Dad's voice isn't coming from outside here, though. It's somewhere off to the left, which makes me think he's probably on the lawn in front of the house, or even standing out on the street, though that's less likely because he wouldn't be able to see over the high, thick hedge. I can hear the words he's shouting now very clearly:

"Just come out and talk to me, you heartless bitch! That's all I want! Just to fucking talk! Can't you at least do that? You fucking owe me that! You took my fucking kids and left me with nothing, so you *fucking owe me!*"

He almost screeches the last few words, though it's not this that makes my heart lurch. It's his reference to his kids, to me and Angie. For a weird moment I almost feel like he can see us or at least sense us.

I instinctively want to hide, to keep low, but Angie is striding towards the corridor on our left, and so I go after her. I feel like a dog on a lead, being tugged along by its owner.

The first door on the right is a little kitchen and the second door leads into a big communal sitting room with lots of mismatching armchairs and settees that are old and squashy, but really comfortable. There's a colour TV in here, but it doesn't get very good reception on ITV, and a record player that's hardly ever used. There's also a big bay window which looks out over the front lawn, covered in wire mesh like all the other ground floor windows to protect it from flying missiles.

The door is slightly ajar. When Angie pushes it, we hear voices. As we step into the room the door creaks and the figures gathered around the window turn round. There are at least six of them, maybe eight. It's hard to tell because they're standing in the dark. I wonder why and then immediately realize: it's because they don't want to be seen from the outside.

I assume one of the figures (who are all women) is Mum, but I don't locate her until she speaks. Her voice is an angry hiss, but it's also wavery, as if she's scared or upset. "What are you two doing here?"

I leave it to Angie to answer. It's because of her that we're here, after all.

"We want to see Dad," she says.

Realising that this might be misunderstood I add quickly, "Not see him to talk to. Just see what he's doing."

Mum shakes her head. "I don't want you here. I want you to go back to bed."

But Angie stands her ground and shakes her head stubbornly. "I don't want to. I want to stay."

Another of the women speaks. I realize it's Mrs Hardy. Linda. Gently she says, "Your mother's upset, Angie. She doesn't want you seeing this. She doesn't want *you* getting upset as well."

"We're not upset," Angie says. "Are we, Frank?"

"Er... no," I say.

"All the same," says Mrs Hardy, "I'm not sure that it's suitable-"

Angie cuts in. I'm amazed by her rudeness. "We used to get upset when Dad hurt Mum, but Dad shouting doesn't upset us. We want to be here with Mum in case *she* gets upset. We don't want her to be on her own."

"She's not on her own," one of the other women says. I think it's Mrs Salmon, who's a black lady. "We're here with her."

"It's not the same," Angie says. "We're her family."

They have to raise their voices because Dad's shouting again. He's screaming out Mum's name and shouting, "Can you see me, you bitch? Can you fucking see me?"

I look beyond the ladies, who are standing to one side of the window, half-hidden behind one of the long curtains, which has been pulled back. Although I get a sense of movement I can't see Dad at first, because he's as dark as the hedge behind him. I move forward as quietly as I can so that I can see better. And then as my eyes adjust I pick him out. He's sort of stumbling from side to side, looking up at the house. I ask a question, but Dad's still yelling. "Look at me, you bitch! Look at me!"

Mrs Salmon asks, "What was that, dear? Did you say something?"

Feeling self-conscious I raise my voice a little, just enough to be heard. "What's he got in his hand?"

It's Mrs Hardy who answers. "It's a bag of some sort. We think it might be a briefcase."

Mum says, "George doesn't have a briefcase."

And then Angie, who I haven't noticed gliding up to stand at my shoulder, says, "It's not a briefcase, it's a can."

I'm confused. My first thought is of a tin, the kind that has baked beans or soup in it. Then Mrs Hardy breathes, "Oh God."

"What?" asks one of the ladies, her voice shrill with alarm. "What's the matter?"

"The girl's right, it *is* a can," Mrs Hardy says. Her voice is quiet, but it sends a chill down my back. "It's bloody petrol. He's got petrol with him."

There are gasps and moans of shock. Mum says, "Let me talk to him," and Mrs Hardy says, "Absolutely not. You're not putting yourself in harm's way." While they're arguing I look at Angie and her eyes are wide like an owl's.

"He's going to try to burn the house down," she says in a kind of wonder. "With us in it."

But as if to prove her wrong, Dad suddenly lifts up the can in both hands and turns it upside down. I see a silvery gleam as liquid spills out over his head and clothes. I even think I hear a faint splashing and glugging sound, but maybe I imagine that.

Then he throws the can aside and I definitely *do* hear a muffled clank as it lands on the grass.

"You see what you've made me do?" he yells as if Mum is controlling his movements. "You see what you've brought me to, you bitch?"

"Oh God," Mrs Hardy says, and turns to one of the other women. "Rose, go and dial 999 again. Tell them we need an ambulance and a fire engine as well." One of the knot of women nods and hurries away and Mrs Hardy turns to Mum. "Don't worry, it's only a precaution. I'm sure he's bluffing. Besides, the police will be here any minute."

Dad's still screaming. "You did this, Pat! You did this!"

There's a collective, high-pitched whoop of alarm, even a few small screams, as Dad's wet, gleaming face suddenly appears in the darkness of the garden. It's as if he's got an orange light-bulb in his head, which somebody has just switched on. Then I realize he's holding a cigarette lighter in his hand. I see a tulip-shaped flame flickering in front of him. His eyes are wild, his mouth twisted into a leer.

"Do you want me to do this?" he screams. "Is that what you want? Do you want me to-"

Whenever I think about what happened then I always picture a tiger. That's what it looks like — a huge, orange tiger leaping out of the tiny flame in Dad's hand and pouncing on him. It seems to have the weight of a tiger too, judging by how Dad stumbles and then falls backwards. And then the tiger's gone and Dad is just on fire. He's on fire all over. He's not just burning, he's *raging.*

I'm vaguely aware of activity around me — of woman running and screaming. "*George! George!*" I hear someone screech, but it's only later that it occurs to me it must have been Mum. I'm cushioned by shock. It's like I'm coated in a thick, invisible, numbingly cold layer of rubber. I stare at Dad, but he's not my Dad any more. He's just fire, in the centre of which a black stickman writhes and twists.

I look away from him only once when something bumps against my arm. Glancing to my left I see my sister, Angie. Her face is lit by the flames that are devouring our father. She is completely expressionless, but there is something like rapture in her eyes.

*

Albion Fay is a fantasy, a place that doesn't exist. It is a dream I once had, a story I once read, a false memory.

There have been times over the years when I have believed this;

times when Albion Fay and all that came after has seemed like the delusions of a mad man. I have lain in bed at night, staring into the darkness and wondering if any of it is real. I have even wondered if *I* am who I think I am. Do the insane *know* they're insane? Do they ever doubt the veracity of their experiences, their memories? Do they wake each morning expecting to resume the life they imagine they have always lived only to find that the world has shifted out of true and that they have been plunged into a nightmare?

Four days after the funeral of my brother-in-law and my two nieces I get into my car and drive back to my childhood. I have no sat nav to guide me, no A-Z, no Google maps. A computer search for 'Albion Fay' proves fruitless. I do not even remember the name of the woods or the nearby village. And yet as the late afternoon settles into early dusk I find myself on familiar roads. Memory and instinct have led me here, and perhaps something else; perhaps the bond with my twin has remained strong, after all. Perhaps, by reaching back through the years I have rediscovered it. Who knows? Some say madness and inspiration are flip sides of the same coin.

The sign is gone and the entrance to the dirt road is almost obliterated by foliage, but I find it without hesitation. Even though Albion Fay has haunted me for almost forty years, it feels like coming home. As I bump down the track, hedges and trees squeezing against the car on either side, skeletal branches stretching out to scrape at the windows, the past four decades dissolve as if they are nothing but an illusion, and once again I am gripped by the child-like certainly that a secret line has been crossed, that a veil has been lifted, that I am descending into a realm that is fecund with wildness and powerful magic.

As the road widens slightly and the familiar stone wall at the base of the sloping garden comes into sight on my left, I deliberately avert my eyes. I concentrate on steering the car into the natural layby on the right-hand side, which borders the woods. I turn off the engine and the growling of the car is replaced by what at first seems like silence, but which, after a subtle readjustment of the senses, I recognize as the wordless, almost subliminal whispering of the trees.

The sound is so familiar that I feel ripples of what I can only describe as nostalgic dread scurry through my body and across my skin. *Just the wind* I tell myself, but I grip the steering wheel tightly as though afraid that something might attempt to tear me away from that which is solid and real and comforting, from that which links me to the reliable, humdrum world that I know and trust.

For a moment, as I brace myself for the ordeal ahead, for the flood of memories that I am afraid will overwhelm me, I stare at my hands, the knuckles standing out like a glare of white bone beneath the barest covering of skin, and all at once I am gripped by the sensation that I am the ghost of my father, or perhaps that he is the ghost of me.

The notion appalls me so much that I release my grip on the steering wheel, my hands springing open. Without further delay I open the car door and step out.

As I straighten I turn to take my first look at the house. It is a ruin. The garden is overgrown, the fruit trees a sprawl of dead branches, the wooden platform sagging and rotten. The windows of the house are mostly without glass and the roof has slumped inward like a soufflé that has failed to rise. Even the stone work is flaking and crumbling like dry skin. My eyes flicker briefly to the right and I see that the caves beyond the house are unchanged. They stand timeless and seemingly oblivious to the elements. Their many black eyes regard me with a dead, impenetrable, shark-like stare.

I lift my head in defiance, or perhaps to show that I am no longer the scared and vulnerable boy I once was. But the gesture is futile; the caves, and more especially whatever resides in them, are unmoved.

The wooden gate in the wall is no longer there; now it is simply a gap. I step through and find that the steps up to the house, although choked by undergrowth, are still negotiable. As I slowly ascend the sky seems to deaden and a stillness settles around me. When one of the steps emits a loud creak, the sound so closely resembles a whimpering dog that I look over my shoulder, my heart pounding. Of course there is nothing there, but it doesn't change the sense I have that I am not only awaited, but expected.

I hesitate at the top of the steps, wondering whether the platform will take my weight. But it seems to me there is a sense of ceremony to this reunion; I cannot believe it will end so ignominiously, with the wooden platform collapsing beneath me. And so I step up on to the decking and walk across it to the door of the house that leads directly into the kitchen. The door is standing ajar, as if to make this process as easy as possible.

Stepping into the kitchen I get no sense that the house is occupied. It is nothing but a shell, a body without a soul. Everything is gone — the furniture, the kitchen cupboards, the light fittings. Even the paper has been stripped from the walls, leaving nothing but bare grey plaster beneath.

It is the same story throughout the house. My footsteps echo hollowly as I move from room to room, but there is nothing to see here, nothing to be gleaned. There aren't even any signs of temporary occupation. There is no graffiti on the walls, no discarded condoms, no cigarette butts, no wine bottles. Oddly I don't even find animal leavings; it is as though the building has been shunned. As I descend the stairs after exploring the upper floor I become aware that the shadows which fill this place are getting heavier, darker. There is nothing sinister in this, I tell myself. It is simply late afternoon. The sun is going down.

Exiting the house I see that dusk is causing the caves to lose a little definition. Shadows proliferate, blackness seeping from the cave openings. Or perhaps it is the other way round; perhaps the rock face is camouflaging its apertures by concealing them within shadows of its own. Either way, I can't shake off the notion that the rock is attempting to protect itself, which only strengthens my resolve.

Without hesitation I approach and enter the caves via the triangular entrance that Angie selected on our first full day here. I have a torch, but I don't use it. Neither do I call out my sister's name. I can't deny that I'm scared, that my heart is beating so hard I feel the relentless punch of it pulsing in my throat. But I keep moving forward, my toes probing for solid ground as darkness compresses around me, my fingertips brushing the walls.

Eventually, when there are only glints and slivers of light left, the ground begins to slope upwards. I trudge on, accessing my memories to picture the structure and layout of the cave ahead. Here on my left is the ledge where Angie waited when I went back to the house to fetch a torch (and which had been vacated upon my return); beyond it is the rubbly downward slope, leading to the side tunnel that eventually opens out into the chamber with its trickle of a stream running along the valley floor and its cave-riddled wall, like a vast rabbit warren, over on the far side.

I find the tunnel with my hands and slip into it. I move more slowly now, my toes probing ahead, fearful of going too far and stumbling over the edge and down the jagged slope of the valley beyond. It is not a sheer drop, but it is fairly treacherous all the same; I could easily fall and break a leg. When I feel a cool, steady breeze flowing across me, coming from my left, I stop, knowing that I have arrived.

Just as I did almost four decades earlier, I lower myself to the ground. The stone is so cold beneath me that it feels wet, but I cross my legs and wait. Darkness presses against my eyes like cold fingers and so I close them. Oddly, although I could see nothing before I did so, my other senses immediately seem more acute. I smell the rock and the water below. I hear a steady, distant drip and tiny muscular crackles from my head and shoulders whenever I take a breath.

Time flows by, and yet at the same time it seems suspended. When I hear movement it feels both as though days have passed and as though no time has elapsed at all. The movement takes the form of a slithering and a scuffling along the rock wall, heading in my direction. As it gets louder and closer I hear a panting too and the sound of something sniffing the air, seeking me out. I feel strangely calm. I feel as though the circle is finally closing, as though this is how it should be. I slip my hand into my pocket and close it around the torch, but I will neither switch it on nor open my eyes until the last moment.

There's no need. I already know what I'm going to see.

✻

✳

SNOWBOOKS HORROR NOVELLAS

THE BUREAU OF THEM

Cate Gardner

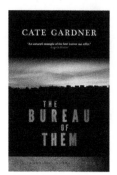

You're not the first to talk to your dead here, the vagrant said.

The living always chase after their dead until they come upon their own.

Formed from shadow and dust, ghosts inhabit the abandoned office building, angry at the world that denies them. When Katy sees her deceased boyfriend in the window of the derelict building, she finds a way in, hoping to be reunited. Instead, the dead ignore, the dead do not see and only the monster that is Yarker Ryland has need of her there.

SCOURGE

Gary Fry

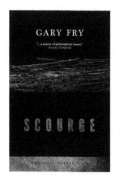

Felachnids: a race of mythical creatures that are rumoured to live in the dark Yorkshire countryside.

The yellow eyes, the double-jointed limbs, the heads that turned backwards whenever that was necessary. These creatures, which otherwise resembled humans, appeared to occupy a small village in North Yorkshire called Nathen.

And Lee Parker is determined to track them down.

THE NINE DEATHS OF DR VALENTINE

John L Probert

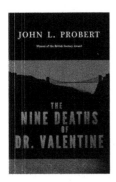

Someone is killing doctors in the style of the murders in Vincent Price movies, leaving the Bristol police baffled. The only man who could possibly be responsible died years ago... or did he... ?

The police in Bristol have been confronted by a series of the most perplexingly elaborate deaths they've ever encountered in all their years of murder enquiries. The only thing which connects them is their seemingly random nature and their sheer outrageousness. As Detective Inspector Longdon and his assistant Sergeant Jenny Newham (with the help of pathologist Dr. Richard Patterson) race against time to find the murderer, they eventually realise that the link which connects the killings is even more bizarre than any of them dared to think...

Lightning Source UK Ltd.
Milton Keynes UK
UKOW06f0645230617
303809UK00009B/181/P